THE CART MASSACRES

John Robert Cameron

CONTENTS

The megalopolis of Hanmer began as an unremarkable hamlet in the depths of Northern Ontario, Canada. The township was founded in 1904. Unable to outpace the growth of the larger communities surrounding it, Hanmer was eventually gobbled up by the larger town of Valley East in 1969. As big fish must prey upon the small, Valley East, too, eventually fell victim to the much larger city of Sudbury. In 2001, the city of Greater Sudbury was born: an amalgamation of vast regions totalling nearly 4,000 square kilometres, yet home to a scant 150,000 souls.

General directions to Hanmer for most people in the Americas: Head north. Make your way to Toronto. When you get there, take Highway 400 and keep going north. Once you see Sudbury's Superstack spewing smoke over the horizon, feel free to admire all the unnatural beauty. Unless you're the one driving, in which case you should probably pay attention to the multitude of potholes. Continue driving through the city of Greater Sudbury. You may feel that the city seems to sprawl on endlessly. You're not imagining things. It kind of *does*.

What direction should you go?

North.

Always north.

Follow Paris Street. Ignore the decrepit hospital painted in bleeding rainbows and butterflies. Why is that monstrosity there, you ask? Fuck if *I* know. Because you're in *Sudbury,* where people accept the idiocy foisted unto them, I guess. Drive north for thirty more minutes. Go through Val Caron, past Val Therese, then 'round the bend.

You've reached Hanmer.

General guide for anyone outside of the Americas:

Find your way to the Americas. Follow the above directions.

For many years, Hanmer was destined to languish in the long shadow of Sudbury's Superstack: a massive, free-standing smokestack the height of the Empire State Building. Going into full operation in 1972, the chimney spewed forth the filthy residue of nickel-rich ore smelting. It sent the poison high, high up into the atmosphere, where the winds carried it far away from Sudbury. This did wonders for the local environment; the deadly mix of sulphurous gas became everyone else's problem, in a more diluted dosage. The Superstack was briefly the tallest freestanding structure in Canada until the massive erection of Toronto's CN Tower.

The heralding event of Hanmer's uprising and metamorphosis from tiny town to megalopolis occurred in 2022. The year started innocuously enough: babies were born, fights were fought, and games were won and lost. People concerned themselves with their lives.

As was the case in many small towns of the time, Hanmer had two grocery stores: one in the good part of town, and one in the bad. The store in the bad part of town was, well, simply put... bad. Wilted vegetables lay dormant on the shelves, rank of rot. The meat was rarely fresh. When decent-quality beef did make it to the back of the store, it certainly didn't get into the hands of the customers. The butchers took it home for themselves. The floors were dingy, scuffed, discoloured, and sticky.

There was a weekly five-dollar special on whole, fresh, raw

chickens. Every Sunday night, the birds that hadn't sold during the week vanished from the shelf, along with a large bottle of vinegar and a sponge. Discounted chickens went out for sale Monday mornings.

Despite all its shortcomings, the store was always busy.

The grocery carts were in terrible shape. They'd been abused, beaten, kicked, clipped by cars, and ridden by teens. Most of them littered the parking lot and the cart corral, though carts could also be sporadically found several kilometres from the store in every direction. The carts seemed to spontaneously concentrate themselves in clusters near the entrances of heavily subsidized housing communities. Canadian scientists have studied this bizarre phenomenon endlessly with no conclusive results. An inquiry into the matter was launched by the Government of Canada. The greatest bureaucracy in the world expects the results of the inquiry sometime before fall of 2028, and promises to solve this problem by 2043. Singleton carts could turn up anywhere. In the depths of winter, sometimes you'll see them peeking out of two-metre-high snowbanks. Carts can turn up as far as people are willing to push them.

The other grocery store in town was clean and smelled fresh. Its employees were paid a trifle more than minimum wage, which made a tremendous psychological difference. They all realized that working for minimum wage was no different than legal enslavement. Hanmerites who made this realization were more likely to reside in the good side of town, so they could shop at the good grocery store. The good grocery store wasn't centrally located within the good side of town, as was the bad one in the bad part of town. Rather, the good grocery store was on the very fringe of town, as far away from the bad part of town as it possibly could be.

This made sense to the well-to-do people, because they didn't want to shop with the poor people. The common conception was that *all* poor people took poorer care of themselves. It was a hard misconception to shake, particularly when someone stands beside you wearing a heavy winter coat that's absorbed a thousand cartons' worth of cigarette smoke. The coats were never washed — just worn, until they were as worn out as the people wearing them. The less-well-to-do people (who lived closer to the poor people than the truly-well-to-do people) were perfectly content driving the farther distance to the good grocery store, despite the bad grocery store being closer.

Hence, a lot of bad-smelling people went to the bad-smelling grocery store. Some of them, particularly the elderly, could be forgiven for their foul odour. Less forgivable were the younger Canucks that simply drank too much rye, smoked anything they could get their hands on, didn't brush their teeth, take showers, or any combination thereof.

Every day people came to the store, bought their groceries, and left. If they wanted more than a few bags of groceries and didn't have a car, they'd usually just walk off with the grocery cart, abandoning it somewhere near their home. At the time, this was commonly considered to be a "victimless crime." The store's owner, Little Jim McGee, suffered the expense of having two stock boys round up carts in a pickup truck every night.

Jim McGee grew up in one of those aforementioned bad-part-of-town subsidized apartments. He'd started working at the store as a bag boy for minimum wage while he was in high school. His boss was a prick to all his employees.

Jim was no exception.

-2-

L ittle Jim hadn't always been called Little Jim. Once upon a time, he was just Jim. While he'd always been smaller than the other children in his class, he hadn't yet been labelled with this permanent prefix. During his first day in fifth grade, a day he would never forget, he met the boys' gym teacher, Mr. Pecante.

Mr. Pecante arrived at Jim's class immediately after they'd finished their math lesson. He had bright blue eyes, with nary a hair anywhere on his head save his blond eyelashes, and even blonder, thick, bushy eyebrows. He shaved his scalp clean twice a day with a straight-edge razor that he carried on him at all times, rather than let the halo of male-pattern baldness creep through. He wore a white, tight muscle shirt, and the stark white bottom half of a martial arts ghi. A bright green fanny pack, far larger than anyone would consider practical, hung from his waist. His shiny gold whistle dangled from his neck, swaying back and forth, mesmerizing the impressionable children.

He told the boys to grab their gym clothes and line up in the hallway.

In fourth grade, Jim and his classmates weren't required to change their clothes for gym. That meant a lot of rank-smelling children, but saved many a teacher the worry of being accused of anything inappropriate, since some tykes still couldn't manage to get on their own shoes, let alone their underwear, prior to the fifth grade.

Jim would grow up hating Mr. Pecante, not because Mr. Pecante was a terribly bad guy, but because for the next four years Mr. Pecante would come to represent everything in the world that Jim was horrible at. Mr. Pecante never knew he'd done wrong by Jim. He just went through the paces, doing his best with the boys. Such was the normal rigour of the gym teacher.

On that fateful first day he greeted the new boys in their classroom, his head glistening beneath the sterile bright lights of the public school. He led the boys away from their class, single file. His baggy ghi pants swished, his fanny pack jingled, and the golden whistle swayed back and forth across his chest as he strode. Down the hallways they went into uncharted territory towards the senior gymnasium. The boys shuffled along behind him with their gym clothes in hand, like fresh inmates nervously following a guard on the first day of prison.

Mr. Pecante eventually stopped at a red door and turned to face the boys. He gestured fancifully towards it, announcing, "Door, meet Mrs. Richardson's class! Door, say hello." Mr. Pecante made a funny face, looked to the ceiling, and squeaked, "*Hello, boys!*" He gave the kids a toothy grin. None of the boys smiled back. Undeterred, he continued, "Boys, say hello to the change room door!"

Three of the children rolled their eyes, four shuffled their feet, six sighed, and a handful feigned smiles. Of all those, two weakly said, "Hi, door." One of them was Jim. The other misfit was Jim's best friend, Julian.

Julian was physically and mentally handicapped. The handicap that had the least impact on Julian, but perhaps the most impact on others, was a general disfigurement of his face.

A trench ran from the upper right of his forehead to the bottom left of his chin. Luckily for Julian, he'd never get a nickname the way Jim would.

Although in one alternate universe, where Julian had been named George, the kids called him "Gorge-y George-y". Had Julian's parents in *this* universe also named him George, it would have at least given him occasional respite from incessantly being called "retard." The other boys often ganged up on Julian and Jim during recess — surrounding them, chanting the slur. Jim would just look down and away. While he wouldn't leave Julian's side during these assaults, he also never intervened.

Jim was fairly intelligent, but proportionately small in all regards. His head was small, his hands were small, his feet were small, even his eyes were small: a true and proper homunculus. It wasn't difficult to see why he never stepped between his friend and the mob.

In the hallway, Mr. Pecante continued, "In you go, and out you come. Change into your shorts, shirts, and socks. Save your clean skivvies for after gym."

The boys looked confused. One timidly asked, "Skivvies?"

"Your underwear, fellas." He pulled out a key and opened the door.

The change room was well lit, aside from one fluorescent tube that flickered steadily, buzzing and pinging.

Mr. Pecante held the door open with his backside and draped his arm across the open doorway. The boys filed in under his arm, one by one. Jim and Julian went in last, and returned first.

Mr. Pecante stood with his arms crossed, smiling brightly, making infrequent eye contact with Jim and Julian while the rest of the boys trickled out. When the last of them arrived, he led his class into the nearby gymnasium. Doubling as the school's auditorium, it had a large stage embedded into the far wall.

Mr. Pecante walked to the stage, turned his back to it, planted his palms on the ledge, and hoisted himself up. He shimmied into a comfortable position, letting his legs dangle. The boys gathered near him, and he told them to sit. They planted their butts onto the freshly polished floor.

Jim looked up. His new teacher seemed very, very far away. He watched Mr. Pecante take a straight-edge razor from his fanny pack, along with a giant red apple. Mr. Pecante delicately peeled the apple, round and round, turning it in one hand, keeping the blade steady in the other. He slowly skinned it, making a perfectly consistent, thin ribbon.

The peel was nearly a foot long when he said, "Today we're going to have fun, boys. *I* certainly think so, anyhow. Gym doesn't have to be difficult. Some of you will be better than others, just like in all your other subjects. But here, if everyone tries and sweats, everyone passes. That's all I ask. We're going to make a great team, eh?" The red ribbon was nearly two feet long, the apple half peeled. "Who here wants a piece of this?"

All the boys raised their hands.

Mr. Pecante finished peeling the apple and held the organic spring aloft. It spindled most of the way to the floor. He flicked his wrist, commanding the spring to retract. It bounded back up into his hand, then he tossed it beside him like a dead snake.

He cut up the apple, handing out thin slices as he freed them from the core. Jim and Julian, as usual, were the last of the outstretched grubby hands to be served. Only a sparingly slim slice remained of the whole. Mr. Pecante began carefully dividing what little was left.

Jim sighed and withdrew his hand. Mr. Pecante nodded to Jim and offered the full slice to Julian.

Julian snatched it, opened his lopsided mouth and devoured it eagerly.

Mr. Pecante tossed the core atop its peel, wiped the blade down on his pants, folded it up and placed it back into his fanny pack. Then he took his whistle, giving it a short, piercing blast.

The class ran laps. Jumped jacks. Squatted squats. Ran more laps. Pushed push-ups. Ran more laps. After about twenty minutes of that routine, every boy gasped for air.

The whistle screamed. Mr. Pecante divided them into two teams, making sure to split up Julian and Jim so neither team suffered much more than the other. Then he dropped from the edge of the stage, planting his feet on the gym floor with a satisfying whump. He went to the equipment closet and pulled out a pair of grey foam balls, tossing one to Julian and the other to Jim. Mr. Pecante figured it might be the only time in the game they'd get a chance to throw. He was a nice teacher like that. Always thinking ahead. He explained the rules of dodgeball to the kids, sat back on the stage, and blew the whistle.

Jim watched as Julian held the ball at his side, unsure of himself. He would have made easy, slow prey. Instead, Jim edged close to the centre line, picked another target, and whipped the ball as hard as he could. It sailed steadily, on course.

The other boy swiftly snatched the ball out of the air.

Mr. Pecante blew the whistle and pointed at Jim. "You're out, little guy!"

"It's Jim, sir," he called back. Just as he started walking off the court, he got drilled in the side of the head by one of the balls. He turned to see Julian, empty-handed, laughing and cheering.

Everyone else in the class laughed, too.

Mr. Pecante wanted to laugh, but couldn't, because he was the teacher. He'd laugh about it later with all the other teachers in the staff room.

Jim's face reddened. He grit his teeth and ignored it, sitting out the remainder of the game at the foot of the stage. More games of dodgeball followed. Jim and Julian would get knocked out quickly and they'd sit side by side beneath the dangling legs of Mr. Pecante.

At the end of the rigorous period, Mr. Pecante blew his whistle, then led the boys back to the change room. In the boys went. The flickering light buzzed and pinged above. Jim and Julian stood side by side, as always. Jim, who'd purposefully picked a spot in the corner of the room beforehand, faced towards it while he removed his shorts and underpants. He tried to keep the others from seeing; the others, for their part, kept to themselves. No one with any sense wanted to be caught looking at anything that wasn't theirs, anyway.

The words were uttered innocently enough, by a rather stupid boy with a disfigured cranium. Peering over Jim's shoulder, Julian quietly said, "Geez, Jim. It's so little, just like the rest of you."

One of the other boys overheard Julian's comment and turned to look. He shouted, "Hey everyone! Little Jim's got a little jimmy! A *really* little jimmy!" The entire class tried to see, crowding inward on him.

Jim didn't know what to do. He hurriedly dressed himself. When the laughing faded, the nickname, tossed upon the wind amidst the normal silence of communal discomfort, started getting chanted by the entire class.

"Lit-tle Jim-my!" "Lit-tle Jim-my!" "Lit-tle Jim-my!"

No corner in any dimension could hide him. It was a dank, rank place to be trapped. Even Julian joined in. He laughed and pointed like the rest of them.

"Lit-tle Jim-my!" "Lit-tle Jim-my!" "Lit-tle Jim-my!"

Jim welled with tears and filled with rage. He tensed up and punched Julian in the face with every minuscule muscle he could muster.

The other kids watched the cripple crumple. Julian took a header into the wooden bench, then crashed to the cement floor in a heap of twisted limbs.

The chanting ceased.

The light buzzed and pinged.

When Jim returned from his two-week suspension, he didn't have any friends left, and would never make new ones. From then on, everyone, including most of his teachers, called him Little Jim, or Little Jimmy, or Jimmy, or retard, or something else. Anything other than Jim. He hated being called Little. He hated being called Jimmy. He hated being called Little Jimmy. He hated being Little Jimmy. After punching out Julian, the principal had threatened Jim with expulsion should he have another outburst. Little Jimmy grew up harbouring a great deal of pent-up resentment towards everyone and everything.

Since Jim didn't talk much to his co-workers at the store, go on smoke breaks, take long lunches, show up late, or call in sick, his boss quickly promoted him from bag boy to stock boy. Soon, he was the head stock boy, and eventually, the manager. He worked hard for years, saved his money (since he had no friends to spend it on or with) and bought the store, allowing his prick of a boss to retire. He renamed the store Little Jim's, despite his reservations about the nickname. No one would ever care enough to ask why he did that. Had they, he'd have simply answered: "It's too difficult to rebrand now. Better the devil you know." Business was business. The irony was that the moment the store changed hands, people (particularly his staff) stopped calling him "little."

At least to his face.

-3-

It's prudent at this time to introduce Big Jesse McGee, Little Jim's nephew, who'd recently graduated from Laurentian University. Big Jesse was called Big Jesse because he was exactly that. He was an honest six-and-a-half feet tall, broad, and built like a transport. He didn't mind being called "big." Jesse plodded slowly (when there wasn't an excuse to run), careful of his footing, always looking down.

His time on the football field was an entirely different matter. You wouldn't think someone so big could move so swiftly. In high school, he'd been the team's star running back. Locals had no idea that such a talent resided in their midst: bleachers on game days were usually empty. Most Canadians only watched the Super Bowl for the half-time show, funny commercials, and an extra excuse to get drunk on a Sunday afternoon. The only thing Canadians cared less about than the National Football League was the Canadian Football League.

Jesse glided through life on good looks and a little bit of innocent charm. During his high school days, more than one teacher gave him an undeserved passing grade at the coach's request so he could keep playing football. He'd even won a scholarship to play for Laurentian University, which had nothing better to do with its money. As the first of his family to ever attend a post-secondary institution, Jesse insisted on being punctual for his nonsense liberal arts classes. This was much to the frustration of his professors, who had better things to do than repeatedly repeat things to him, and to his coaches, who preferred he spend more time practicing and memorizing plays.

After five short years of football, he was awarded a useless degree that left him entirely unemployable. He attended a try-out for the Canadian Football League but failed to make it through the last cut. Something to do with never being able to remember what play the quarterback had just called.

Since Big Jesse didn't typically make very good decisions, and since he certainly wasn't going to ask the advice of anyone who might, he did what many other people do, have done, and will continue doing: flipping a quarter to determine whether or not he'd keep pursuing a career in football. The coin landed heads. He hung up his helmet and asked his Uncle Jim for a job at the grocery store.

On the Flip Side:

All choices create new forks in the road.

In an alternate universe, the quarter landed tails, which (on a Canadian coin) is a picture of a caribou. But not this coin. This coin bore the image of George Washington, because Canadians often use American and Canadian coins interchangeably.

Americans always manage to creep into the mix somehow.

In the alternate universe, Big Jesse recovers from his failure and finds a path to the NFL, where he gets converted into one of the most dependable defensive tackles in the game, helping the Arizona Cardinals win an unprecedented four consecutive Super Bowls. Defensive tackles don't have to remember plays.

Their only assignment is to knock down the guy with the ball any which way they can. After retiring, he'd get addicted to hard drugs and push his pregnant girlfriend down a flight of stairs.

Luckily, as far as *we're* concerned, in *our* little speck of the multi-cosmos, none of those things happen, happened, or are going to happen.

Back to Reality:

When Big Jesse arrived unannounced at Little Jim's Grocery Store, Jim figured he had little choice but to employ his nephew. Not wanting to burden any department with him, Jim made Jesse a bag boy, isolating him from the rest of the staff. Little Jim hadn't actually had a bag boy working for him since he bought the store and fired them all. Jim told the cashiers to work harder and help customers bag their own groceries. This meant he expected the customers to work harder, too, though he never said that to their faces.

After hiring Big Jesse, Little Jim quickly noticed that many of his customers were creating absurdly long lines at whichever cash Jesse was bagging. The queue consisted entirely of the elderly and the infirm who didn't mind waiting for the additional service. Jim saw to hiring a second bag boy to clean up the mess his nephew was making. Jesse kept costing him money. Jim's hiring process was very simple: when he needed someone, he'd wait for the next person to walk in seeking work, interview them on the spot, and hire them if they suited his desires.

A day later, a young man named Horatio happened into the store, job application in hand. I won't go into too much detail about him; because he's going to die shortly, there's just not much reason to.

I suppose, if you *must* know what he looked like (it might help you envision his death), he was very plain looking. Many shades of brown he was: brown eyebrows, brown eyes, brown hair, and brown skin. Not particularly tall, not particularly short, not particularly thin, and not particularly fat. Unremarkable in all respects.

From the comfort of his office, Jim watched on the security monitor as the boy came into the store with obvious purpose. Horatio approached the courtesy counter, application in outstretched hand. Jim pressed a button on his intercom. "Send the boy back here, Loretta."

Jim's voice echoed throughout the store.

Horatio looked up nervously, instinctively seeking the source. The woman at the desk told him where to go. He made his way to Jim's office. The door was already open. "In, boy, in," Little Jim beckoned.

Horatio stepped inside and looked down at the little man behind the big desk.

"Well? What's your name, boy?"

"Horatio, sir."

"Horatio," Jim mimicked. He saw the flopping piece of paper in the boy's hand. "Is that your resume? Give it here."

Horatio handed it down.

Jim studied the resume, flipping it over from one side of the page to the other. "Uh-huh.... Uh-huh.... Well, that was a stupid field of study. No one's hiring for that."

Horatio smiled nervously and wiped his palms against his

jeans.

"Will you steal from me?" Little Jim snapped.

Horatio stopped smiling. "Sir?" he asked cautiously. "No, sir."

"Any medical problems? Are you going to call in sick next week because your chronic asthma is kicking in?"

Horatio shook his head. "No, sir. No problems. Healthy as an ox."

"Do you smoke?"

Horatio was pretty sure Little Jim wasn't allowed to ask that, but since he didn't smoke, he just answered, "No."

"Good." Little Jim leaned back in his chair, putting his feet up on his desk. "Stinks enough in here already. Lazy fucking staff." He stared at the security screens for a while, mulling it over. "Hmm." He thumbed through the resume some more. "You're hired. You start now or never. Follow me." Little Jim lifted his feet off the desk and stood up, beckoning the boy to follow him into the store, where Jim apprehended Jesse from his bagging duties, leaving an elderly woman to fend for herself. The cashier turned to the woman, giving her a look that very clearly communicated: *Those eggs ain't gonna bag themselves, old lady.*

Jim led both boys on a tour of the store. It was Jesse's second go-around, but Little Jim knew he could use the refresher. Jim showed them the break room, the coolers, and the deli. Then he showed them the cardboard baling press, where a boy wearing a brown apron was tossing in empty cardboard boxes.

"Hey!" Jim yelled at the boy. "How many times do I have to tell you idiots? Flatten the boxes before you put them in. Why am I paying to run this thing more often than I have to? When the boxes aren't flattened, they fill the baler faster, and you have to run it more. Do you have any idea how much it costs to maintain that machine? Flatten them first!"

The boy was stupefied. "But… I can't find my boxcutter."

Jim's little face instantly turned beet red. "WE SELL BOXCUTTERS! GO GRAB A GODDAMN BOXCUTTER OFF THE GODDAMN SHELF AND GODDAMN FUCKING USE IT! BETTER GODDAMNED YET, WHILE YOU'RE GODDAMN AT IT, GO GET SOME GODDAMN TWINE FROM THE GODDAMN DELI, FIND SOME GODDAMN DUCT TAPE, AND TAPE THE GODDAMN BOX CUTTER TO THE GODDAMN BALER, SO YOU GODDAMN MORONS AREN'T WASTING ANY MORE OF MY GODDAMN TIME AND GODDAMN MONEY OVER A GODDAMN TWO-DOLLAR BOXCUTTER!"

The boy's eyes widened. He nodded, dropped the box in his hands, and ran away.

Jesse didn't think much of the event because he'd grown up with his uncle and nothing seemed at all out of order.

Horatio considered running out the emergency exit.

"And you two — don't even touch that machine. Don't so much as throw a box in there. Don't go anywhere near it. That thing can crush a cow into a giant hamburger patty." Jim walked towards the next destination on the tour while he muttered something about insurance and liability.

The boys quickly followed.

You might be led to believe that Horatio dies in that baler, but don't, because he doesn't. Kindly let me foreshadow my own story. Thank you. What's important to realize is that the boys were given a general tour, told to put people's purchases in bags, and watch for shoplifters. Large signs throughout the store and parking lot forbade the practice of shoplifting, threatening shoplifters to the fullest extent of the law. Those signs also forbade the removal of shopping carts from the property of Little Jim's Grocery Store.

Horatio and Jesse filled one plastic bag after another. Some people brought in reusable fabric ones. If the bags stunk, it was usually a safe bet that the people that brought them stunk, too. The boys spent their days retrieving carts from the parking lot, and bagging groceries. It was a safe, if meaningless, existence.

A few months later, one of the stock boys who'd been regularly taking the pickup truck out to retrieve grocery carts complained to Jim about his sore back. "Them sons of bitches are heavy, sir," he told Jim. "Hoistin' 'em up ain't gettin' any easier."

Jim nodded. He knew the perfect team for the job. He reassigned all cart retrieval duties to the bag boys. They did it diligently enough. Bag groceries, retrieve carts from the lot, retrieve carts from the town. Rinse. Repeat. Big Jesse was a natural. The carts looked like mere toys in his hands. Horatio only needed to stand idly in the back of the pickup, cramming carts into the rear slots of the ones in front. One wonders whether the frontmost carts felt jealous, having filled no other carts' slots, or if those in the rear felt relieved that they hadn't been penetrated. Perhaps it was the other way around.

-4-

T ime passed, as it tends to do. Bags were filled with groceries, and carts were endlessly stolen, hunted, retrieved, then stolen again. The regular debauchery of life continued around them. Big Jesse and Horatio spent a lot of time together. Having had enough of the routine, Horatio suggested to Little Jim that they could install GPS tracking devices on the carts to more quickly locate them. Horatio was a pretty smart guy but suffered from having a degree that was just as blatantly bullshit as Jesse's, despite it having been ten times more difficult to earn. Unfortunately for Horatio, he was still a dreamer, uncrushed by the world. All of this is quite sad, because he's going to die soon. Doesn't that make you feel bad? You may have already envisioned him getting mangled in a baling press.

You must be a terrible person.

Little Jim didn't much like people, but he was happy to take good advice when it came his way. He started placing trackers on all the carts that were still in decent shape. He reasoned that this made the most sense, since he'd previously observed that people making off with his carts rarely took old ones with squeaky wheels or warped frames. That would make the carts more difficult to push through all the potholes and mud puddles, not to mention the salty, sandy slush during the seemingly endless winters.

The next time the bag boys went to round up the carts,

they followed the trackers, corralling cart after cart, cluster by cluster. When Horatio zoomed out on the map to check their progress, he was stunned by the location of one cart. "Look at that, Jesse. It's all the way across town, on the outskirts. Why didn't they just go to the other store?"

They sped the pickup out of the bad part of Hanmer, into the not-so-bad part, then into the good part, through the better part of the good part, into the best part, past the good grocery store, and beyond.

They soon came to a long, winding driveway stemming from a side road in the bush, a little ways out of town. It was pitted with deep ruts full of fresh mud from a recent rainfall. Jesse guided the truck in, bumping and grinding down the narrow path. Stray branches jutted out from the bush, scraping the side of the truck as they went by. The carts in the truck bed clacked and banged, back and forth, up and down, and side to side. It was safe to say that the boys' approach was well announced. They pulled up to a large, dilapidated, three-story house, sitting on an unkempt, weedy lot, shrouded on both sides by deep woods. The house had a wheelchair ramp on the side entrance, beneath a covered carport containing the rusted-out frame of a long-ago abandoned pickup truck. Both the ramp and carport looked to be on the verge of collapsing at any moment. They got out of the truck and crept up the creaking ramp to knock at the door. The young woman who answered was a skinny little rail with long, frazzled hair and thinning eyebrows. A cigarette dangled from her parched lips. The sharp cry of pain from an infant within the home didn't appear to bother her in the least.

She took another drag of the cigarette, then blew smoke at the boys. "What?" she demanded. "Children's Aid again? Fuck you guys. What lies did that asshole tell you this time?"

The boys looked at one another, each begging the other to speak first.

Horatio said, "Umm. Well, Miss, we're not from the Children's Aid Society. We're from Little Jim's, and according to the GPS tracker on a cart from our store, it's currently located here."

"Oh." She squinted at the boys. "Well, piss off, anyway." She slammed the door shut.

Jesse looked at Horatio. "That didn't go well."

"No shit, Captain Obvious." Horatio pounded on the door. "Hey! Do you think I'm jerking around? I'll call the cops!" Silence prevailed. "Okay! I'm calling the cops right now!"

The door opened and the frazzled Thin Woman reappeared. "Don't call the cops! Fuckers. Just... fine. Come in. Just... don't mind the mess. Fucking Gestapo, digital Nazi assholes," she muttered. "Follow me."

The inside of the home was complete squalor. The boys winced at the smell of what could only be described as a rancid mix of pickles, diarrhea, and stale urine. The blinds were nearly drawn shut, allowing just the faintest sliver of light to shine through, illuminating the billowing cigarette smoke and dust in the air.

Jesse took a quick look at the floor, assessing whether he'd be asked to take his shoes off. Even in the dimness, he saw the tracks immediately: a thick cake of mud and filth leading through the entranceway and across the stained carpet of the living room. He left his shoes on.

Horatio had never even thought about taking his off.

They were led through the living room, where a decrepit old woman lay on a ratty orange couch. The old woman yelled, in a thick, French Canadian accent, "*Maudit!* And just who're 'dem Anglo fucks, eh? *Câlisse, Tabarnak!* Pas chez *moi!!*" She was surprisingly loud, though neither of the boys understood a single thing she'd said.

The Thin Woman yelled back, "Never-yooooou-fuckin'-mind! Don't get me started on *you*. Don't matter anyhow. Go back to sleep!" She led the boys to the kitchen, where the tracks sidled right up to the counter. The tracks continued from there to the back door. She led the boys out onto a large porch with no railings, six feet off the ground. Behind the house was a large clearing in the woods the size of a small baseball field. It was full of carts. Carts, carts, and more carts. At the back of the yard, there was a dense mass of carts in neat lines. Closer, there were singles and little clusters everywhere. Some upright ones, some not. Some mangled, some...less mangled.

The boys stood there, taking it all in. It just wasn't something you saw every day. The tracks ended at the edge of the porch. They looked down at more carts, fresh from their falls, lying in an awkward pile of twisted, modern art. Some carts were so old that they were little more than crumbling rust. They sat in the furthest corner of the yard, undisturbed for decades. Those closer to the house bore Little Jim's logo. The others bore the logos of his predecessors. Over the course of several days, Jesse and Horatio retrieved the carts one truckload at a time, without incident.

Little Jim didn't press charges. Nothing really shocked him anymore. He just shook his head and counted his blessings. New carts weren't cheap, and they'd retrieved over 1,200 of them in various states of disrepair. When he'd confronted the Thin Woman about it, she confessed that she'd take the bus to Little Jim's and buy a week's worth of groceries for herself, her kids, and her disabled, shut-in mother. Then she'd push the cart home.

The Thin Woman inherited the practice from her mother. As a child, she'd accompany her mom to the grocery store and watch her load a cart full of the cheapest stuff she could buy, stretching her dollars by using the bad grocery store, where the prices on everyday goods were slightly lower. The old woman always had to be a spendthrift, lest her abusive husband not have enough money for the tavern, or herself enough for the bingo. Week after week, year after year, the generational cart theft continued. Typically, they'd shop on Mondays to take advantage of the cheap, fresh-smelling chickens.

Although some of the recovered carts were no longer viable for store use, even those in poor shape were sold for scrap. Horatio's advice had paid off handsomely for Little Jim.

Horatio's involvement was never acknowledged, nor was he promoted, given a raise, or praised in any way, shape, or form for his contribution to Jim's rising fortune.

I wonder if that was on his mind when he died.

When the following Monday rolled around, the Thin Woman reappeared in the store, did her shopping, paid, and pushed her grocery laden cart into the parking lot.

Little Jim wasn't there to see, nor was he paying attention on the security screens. Little Jim was busy getting a blowjob in his office from Loretta, the head cashier. He was trying to relax and get off so he could concentrate on his work.

Loretta, the buxom, middle-aged blond, made the same salary as Tom, the chubby, balding assistant manager who did most of the work in the store.

Tom wasn't overly angry about it, though, since he wasn't the one sucking Little Jim's little dick. Besides, Loretta had sucked Tom's dick a few times over the years, usually after they'd each had a few too many rounds of rye at staff Christmas parties.

"She weren't no hell," as he'd put it.

So, while Little Jim was indisposed, Big Jesse kept a keen eye on the Thin Woman from the moment he saw her walk into the store. When she pushed her cart towards the street, Jesse went out after her. Horatio followed, fearing the worst.

When she rolled the cart off of store property, Jesse yelled, "Hey!"

She didn't turn.

"HEY!" he yelled, louder.

She turned around and flipped him a double bird, bringing it down to finish at her crotch. Then she started thrusting her pelvis out towards him.

"Son of a..." Big Jesse uttered, sprinting towards her.

When she saw the hulking young man coming, she turned tail and started pushing the cart quickly down the sidewalk.

Jesse soon caught up and began wrestling the cart from her.

The Thin Woman reached into a grocery bag and grabbed a large can of Chef Boyardee ravioli, using it to clock Jesse in the side of the head. Momentarily stunned, Jesse stumbled backwards. The Thin Woman grabbed the handlebar and pushed off.

Horatio ran to Jesse's side, helping steady him on his feet. "Jesse, are you okay?"

Jesse's ears rang. He could feel a welt rising on his temple. He stared distantly; his gaze fixed on something beyond sight.

"Don't worry, we'll call the cops, man. She's fucked, now." Horatio took the phone from his pocket and began dialing.

Jesse stared hatefully at the rapidly fleeing Thin Woman. She cast a glance over her shoulder. Seeing that she hadn't been pursued, she paused a moment to look Big Jesse in the eye and blow him a kiss.

Jesse began running as fast and hard as he could.

Her eyes went wide as she quickly realized that she'd tempted fate one too many times. She hurried away, frantically glancing over her shoulder. Her fifty-metre lead dwindled with each passing second. Jesse soon closed the gap, then dove forwards at full speed, cutting her down at the knees. She toppled forward, smashing face first into the handlebar, then again into the concrete sidewalk.

The cart veered off the curb, tipped wildly onto two wheels, and trundled into oncoming traffic. A green sports utility vehicle struck it head on, sending the contents of the cart in several directions. A bag of oranges vaulted upwards, coming to an explosive landing on the windshield of a car passing by in the opposite direction. Oranges, orange chunks, and orange juice all cascaded through the air. A case of Diet Pepsi burst as a bus ran it over. The cans crumpled like bubble wrap: pop, pop, pop. The bus came to a grinding halt, and a gasoline tanker truck that couldn't stop in time rear-ended it. The bus accordioned in the rear, the gasoline tanker jackknifed, and a small red car hit the tanker broadside. The car, a total write-off, ricocheted away, its driver safely enveloped by front and side airbags. Gasoline began trickling onto the street from a small breach in the tanker.

Horatio caught up, assessed the situation, and prudently screamed, "Run, Jesse!" Which they did, leaving all the victims to fend for themselves. But the tanker didn't explode. Police, ambulance, and fire services arrived, along with several tow trucks to pick apart the mess.

The cart-thieving woman suffered severe facial lacerations, a broken jaw, head and neck trauma, and several fractures to her limbs. Eight passengers and the driver from the bus had whiplash, the driver and passenger of the green SUV broke their noses when their airbags deployed, and the driver of the small red car sprained his wrists.

All of the injured were transported by ambulance to Health Sciences North, the only hospital in the City of Greater Sudbury, thirty kilometres away from Hanmer. The Thin Woman was attended to first. The well-trained staff treated her many wounds and applied a full body cast. Thank goodness for publicly funded health care.

The police asked Jesse several questions before taking him into custody. They stuffed him in the back of a Greater Sudbury police cruiser and headed to the city.

Meanwhile, one of the officers continued to question Horatio on the side of the road. The officer was just about finished when a tow truck driver hooked a cable onto the jack-knifed tractor trailer. When the cable tightened, the winch started groaning. Suddenly, the cable snapped and whipped towards Horatio. It lashed out just far enough to slice him in two, right below the waist.

The cop who'd been speaking with him, mere inches on the side of safety, got Horatio's blood all over his nice, previously clean uniform. You should have seen the look on his face. It was pretty priceless.

After sorting through the facts, and with more recent events in mind, the police decided not to lay charges against Big Jesse. They released him, and he took a bus back to Hanmer. The decision to set him free seemed reasonable at the time, though it may have left the boy with the wrong impression.

-5-

J esse foggily returned to work the next day nursing a pretty good concussion, courtesy of the Thin Woman. Someone had called him during the night to tell him something about Horatio, though he couldn't quite remember what that was. He just knew he couldn't afford to miss work, since he was living paycheque to paycheque.

News of the previous day's events had spread through town. Jesse noticed many customers giving him dirty looks, which he tried to ignore. He wondered why Horatio was late for work while he mindlessly bagged groceries until he squished an old man's bread beneath a large bottle of cranberry juice. The cantankerous customer angrily demanded a replacement. Big Jesse ran to the bakery, got him a fresh loaf, then excused himself. He went outside and leaned against the storefront.

From his office, Little Jim observed Big Jesse on the security screens. He watched Jesse leave his perch at the wall to approach a young man in the process of rolling a cart off store property. Little Jim felt his muscles tighten. Words were exchanged between Big Jesse and the young man, who awkwardly filled his arms with grocery bags before walking away. Jesse started pushing the empty cart back to the corral. Little Jim breathed a sigh of relief and was just about to go have a word with his nephew. At that moment, Jesse gave chase to an old fat man sneaking off with a cart on the other side of the parking lot. Little Jim ran out of his office to the parking lot as quickly as his little legs would take him. By the time he got outside, the fat man was sprawled on the ground, his groceries dumped haphazardly around him. Jesse casually rolled the cart back to put it with the others.

Once again, the police were called. Once again, the police were more or less indifferent. They lived on the good side of town and shopped at the good grocery store. As long as no one was being tackled there, things were fine, so far as they were concerned. When Little Jim reviewed the footage from the outside cameras, he couldn't help but laugh. The panicked fat man barely made it a dozen steps before getting taken down. Jesse tackled someone else the next day, and two the day after that. Little Jim watched the clips and saved them. Day after day, fewer customers stole carts, because day after day, Jesse brought some of them to justice.

Cart thieves soon realized that if they left simultaneously, Jesse couldn't possibly catch them all. The first time they organized, five shoppers from a nearby subsidized apartment complex arranged to arrive and leave together. After checking out, they all walked casually with their carts towards cars in the furthest corners of the parking lot. Then, when they couldn't fake it anymore, they bolted for the street. Jesse managed to tackle two of them in quick succession. The other three vanished.

They'd discovered power in numbers.

So, shoppers began gathering at the edge of the parking lot, scattering when the time seemed prudent. Jesse would watch them but do nothing so long as they were still on the store's property. In the beginning, sometimes just a few shoppers would leave at once, taking their chances. Usually, they broke in larger herds. Customers looked at one another tensely, trying to gauge what the others were thinking. Once in a while, someone would jump the gun, misjudging the others' willingness to run. Off they'd go, only to look over their shoulders and see that nobody had followed — nobody but Jesse. He'd appear out of nowhere with a big smile on his face. Customers eventually began leaving at regular intervals every other hour. Usually, the slowest shoppers were the first to get tackled, though sometimes Jesse challenged himself by running down the faster ones.

When the media caught wind of the bizarre Northern affair, it quickly attracted worldwide attention. People travelled from far and wide to let a dumb beast chase after them, risking severe injury. Little Jim capitalized on the situation, launching a website where anyone could stream the action. They sold gaudy T-shirts and other knick-knacks that immortalized some of Jesse's best tackles. Once Little Jim had a taste of that extra revenue stream, he just couldn't get enough action. Jesse had taken to donning his football helmet, at his uncle's request. Little Jim had muttered something about liability and the performance of regular job functions.

One typical Tuesday afternoon, shoppers waited with their carts at that thin line dividing public from private, constantly looking about, waiting for the herd to multiply before they attempted their escape. Jesse paced back and forth in the parking lot, trying to keep an eye on everyone at once.

Horatio asked him, "Why do you keep doing this, Jesse?"

Big Jesse's eye twitched. The moment passed, and Jesse paced on, eyeing all the potential thieves.

"Maybe you have to," Horatio contemplated. "Who knows?" He left Jesse to tend the flock alone.

A crowd of thirty-two waited nervously for the top of the

hour to roll around. No one dared step across the line without the rest of the group. Big Jesse really couldn't keep up with this level of coordinated attack. When the shoppers ran, most got away.

For Little Jim, turning a blind eye to the odd cart disappearing was one thing. Seeing them all vanish simultaneously was a little harder to stomach. He brought Jesse into his office. "How would you feel about me bringing in another bag boy or two? Is it too soon? How are you feeling?"

Jesse shrugged. "Sure. Horatio has been useless lately. He's hardly ever around."

Little Jim looked at his nephew long and hard. "I'll see about getting you some help."

Jim hired a few other ne'er-do-well members of Jesse's high school football team. Most of them had become fat and lazy since Big Jesse went off to play for the university. Jesse asked his old high school football coach to come in and recondition the new hires. The coach was happy to do it because he was a retired public-school teacher and had precious little left to do but wait for death. He took on the task for a weekly $50 food voucher at the store. This was better for Little Jim than paying cash, though he was annoyed that the coach would use the voucher to buy mostly unprocessed food items with the lowest markup, like milk, eggs, meat, and produce. It may seem strange to be annoyed by something so petty, and had the coach been a stranger, Jim might not have minded so much, but as life would have it, the coach was Mr. Pecante, his head as bald and shiny as ever, particularly beneath the bright fluorescent lights in the grocery store. He still wore white ghi pants and a muscle shirt, with that same bright green fanny pack, which was a little worse for wear. The golden whistle still dangled from his neck. He'd taken the high school coaching position a decade after Little Jim graduated from elementary school.

One day, when Coach Pecante was using his voucher to shop, he noticed a large cardboard cut-out of Mr. Clean standing in aisle three, amongst the rest of the cleaning products. When Coach Pecante stood beside his cardboard counterpart, he looked just like Mr. Clean's equally handsome, slightly shorter, older brother. Another shopper thought this was rather entertaining, took a picture, shared it, and it went viral. It came as quite the ego boost to the coach, because, let's be honest, if Mr. Clean's into women, he gets his fair share. I'm not trying to imply that Mr. Clean's *not* into women, *I* just don't think it's fair to judge people in that way or make any assumptions.

-6-

Little Jim came up with a plan to turn the faucet wide open on his new revenue stream. He developed a set of rules for a competitive team-based sport and sought other grocery store owners to create their own teams of bag boys to compete with. Jim oversaw operations as the league commissioner of *The Cart Massacres*. He tasked Coach Pecante with coaching and managing their team, the Northern Ontario Snowshoe Hares.

The Snowshoe Hares' logo was a brown outline of a giant white hare wearing wooden snowshoes, tackling a shopper to the ground, set against a blue background. The cart was tipped forward with several food items flying out, the brands of which would change seasonally based on who bought the advertising. The reason they named the team the Snowshoe Hares was because on snowy winter days, Big Jesse had taken to wearing his snowshoes to chase shoppers down. He'd always performed best during snowstorms when people couldn't get away quickly with their heavy carts, and there were fewer customers braving the weather dividing his attention. Some thought his use of snowshoes to be unsportsmanlike, but Jesse reasoned that if they wanted to bring their own snowshoes, they were more than welcome.

As the league commissioner, Jim would continue his legacy of being hated by everyone, which seems to be the case for every commissioner of every professional sports league, forever.

That may have something to do with incapable, insecure men who love controlling people that are capable of achieving what they never could. But that's not what this story is about, either.

Well... maybe a little.

With no further ado, the original four teams were:

1. The Northern Ontario Snowshoe Hares, out of Hanmer, Ontario.
2. The Vancouver Island Piercers, (or VIPs), out of Port McNeill, British Columbia.
3. The Mid-Albertan Strong, out of Rocky Mountain House, Alberta.
4. The Prairie Pricklers, out of Porcupine Plain, Saskatchewan.

Little Jim's Grocery Store held the very first match, a duel between the Hanmer Hares and the Piercers. It drew an enormous crowd. The local spectators who didn't have a lot of money — but had a little foresight — sat on lawn chairs they'd brought from home. They filled the parking lot and lined the streets surrounding the store. Those with neither money nor foresight sat on the hot pavement under the sun and got baked. Those with money sat in the newly installed, canopied rooftop seating section. Reengineering the store's roof to bear the load had cost Jim a pretty penny, but he considered it a long-term investment. Hot dogs from the rooftop concession stand were made of beef, while the hot dogs down below were made from meat-flavoured tofu, saturated in diarrhea-inducing red dye. The soda down below was under-carbonated, watered down, and never quite cold enough.

Well, you might be thinking, "Who in their right mind would go shopping that day, risking certain injury from two brigades of bag boys?"

That's a perfectly fine question, and if you'd been just a little more patient, I'd have answered it. So, allow me to introduce...

Commissioner Jim McGee's Original Rules of *The Cart Massacres:*

1. There are 250 shoppers in a game.
2. Each shopper has five minutes to fill their cart.
3. No shopper may participate with less than twenty-five kilograms of merchandise.
4. Shoppers pay for their merchandise.
5. Shoppers wait with their carts at the perimeter of the property.
6. Shoppers are released simultaneously and allowed to run.
7. Two opposing teams of twenty-five bag boys vacate the store from the exits of their choice to pursue the shoppers.
8. The team that recovers merchandise with the highest total value wins.
9. Shoppers who have their merchandise recovered forfeit ownership of said merchandise.
10. Merchandise damaged during the recovery process still counts towards a team's recovery total.
11. The contents of a shopper's cart are deemed recovered after a bag boy has disrupted the cart and/ or shopper, and the cart is tipped.
12. The game's designated play area ceases 500 metres from the store. End zones are clearly marked. A variable number of end zones may exist, depending on the roads surrounding the particular store.
13. Shoppers who make it to an end zone are refunded the purchase price of their merchandise and allowed

to keep said merchandise.

14. Each team may utilize one designated coach, each of which has their own battle room, where they may remain in communication with their teams. The coaches also have access to live mapping of each cart in play, as well as information about the contestants and the value of the merchandise they purchased.

People travelled from far and wide, wearing all sorts of ridiculous costumes in the hopes of being one of the chosen 250. Many of the Canadian shopping wannabes had tried and failed to get through the audition stages of "Canadian Idol," "Canada's Got Talent," and "The Amazing Race Canada." Many of the international shopping wannabes had tried their hand (or voice) at their international reality-TV equivalents. Every hotel in the Greater Sudbury region was filled to capacity, with those in Hanmer charging a steep premium. The world's eyes turned to Little Jim's spectacle.

Contestants filled their carts with a variety of goods. Some people, only there for the spotlight, bought large bags of flour, rice, or potatoes to cheaply meet the weight requirement. But Little Jim's store had a decent selection of livingware, kitchenware, toys, and clothing, too. There was even a small electronics department. For the fast runners, there was true temptation to gamble on pricey merchandise. Coach Pecante had been putting the Hares through wind sprints for months. They were ready.

Little Jim stood atop the store, waiting for the last of the shoppers to line up around the property's edge. When they rolled into place, he announced into a microphone, "ON YOUR MARK." His voice boomed over enormous speakers.

The reality-TV rejects got into running postures.

"GET SET."

They looked nervous and excited.

"GO!"

They ran like hell.

Both teams of bag boys came flying out of every door and loading bay.

In terms of opposing team sports, *The Cart Massacres* quickly had the distinction of being one of the least violent, since neither team had reason to attack one another. In that sense, it was sort of like baseball (whenever Jose Bautista wasn't being punched in the face).

The very first person ever tackled during an official Cart Massacre was Mrs. Tannenbaum, who was mostly blind, totally deaf, and chose the wrong day to pick up a fiftieth anniversary cake for herself and Mr. Tannenbaum. She had pushed a cart to the store from their nearby subsidized apartment. She'd approached the property just as 250 carts were pushed past her in the opposite direction. Then she was tackled simultaneously by seven overly eager bag boys from the Piercers who were all determined to be first.

Inside the store, both coaches sat comfortably in their battle rooms, where they had game footage from multiple angles: store security cameras, drone views, player body-cam views, and a blimp view. One of the drones surely could have flown up and delivered the aerial footage, but a drone wouldn't have made nearly so profitable a billboard as the blimp. Coach Pecante keenly watched the game unfold. He balanced his assets: keeping an eye on high valued carts, but not sending his fastest bag boys after them unless it was absolutely necessary, either to recover the merchandise before a Piercers's bag boy did, or to keep the shopper from reaching an end zone with their goods.

The crowd roared with delight each time someone was tackled, and cheered on the shoppers as they hustled to end zones. The costumed victors often did end zone dances or held up things they'd won like trophies. Anything to keep the drones' attention for as long as possible, extending their personal flirtation with fame.

Coach Pecante did his job well, as did his team. The Hares won easily, recovering 57% of receipted sales to the Piercers meagre 26%. Big Jesse was the game MVP, having tackled a giant pink Hi-Liter, an owl, a samurai, a miner, and a Siamese cat.

Of the 250 shoppers' carts, 102 were tipped over. Of those shoppers, 58 walked away in reasonably good shape, went home, and were forever telling the story about how they were toppled in the very first ever — yes, *ever* — Cart Massacre.

The other 44 shoppers clogged the emergency room waiting area at Health Sciences North, where they sat for hours. Most of the staff were busy, urgently trying to save poor Mrs. Tannenbaum. I'll forgive you for assuming she'd died on impact, being so decrepitly feeble and old. Had she been given a quick death, that might have been better for her. Alas, her destiny was to live on, comatose, for a while longer. Incidentally, Mr. Tannenbaum died of a heart attack thirty-eight seconds after she was tackled. He'd been watching the Cart Massacre at the local legion. You're probably thinking he died of a broken heart. That's a nice sentiment. You'd be entirely wrong, though. Mr. and Mrs. Tannenbaum married at a very young age. She went nearly blind and totally deaf shortly thereafter, becoming a terrible burden on Mr. Tannenbaum, who only stayed with her out of an archaic sense of obligation.

He burst out laughing when he saw it happen.

Most of his octogenarian legion buddies didn't quite grasp the humour. They were actually appalled, for Mrs. Tannenbaum was a dear, helpless woman who wouldn't swat a fly. (Not that she could.) They didn't know that Mrs. Tannenbaum had become very good at feigning kindness in public, having quickly realized that being blind, deaf, and miserable didn't generate nearly so much sympathy as did being blind, deaf, and seemingly pleasant. She'd return after outings to natter at her husband, and natter she could, occasionally swinging her cane in his direction, dumping her pent-up rage into the only available receptacle. She'd seen beautiful things, once. She'd been the centre of attention, both in and of conversations. She'd been alive.

Knowing only what he knew, and feeling only what he felt, Mr. Tannenbaum laughed. He witnessed the revolted looks cast upon him by his friends and stopped laughing. Then his face contorted into something ugly, and he promptly had a massive, fatal heart attack. His timely death was his saving grace, since his buddies simply chalked up the fit of hysteria to a last moment's utter madness. Who wouldn't crack, seeing their wife gang-tackled? Some of his buddies were secretly sort of happy to see him go, because Mr. Tannenbaum bet the spread heavily on the home team against them, and the Hares opened it up wide.

On the Flip Side:

In the coin-flip universe, where Big Jesse wins the Super Bowl on four consecutive occasions but none of *this* happens, Mrs. Tannenbaum gets hit by a car on her way home from the store, killing her instantly. That tends to happen to mostly sightless deaf people with cognitive impairment when they wander about. Safe to say, had it not been for the dementia, she'd have known enough to stay home. It was quite inevitable, really. A hit and run. Very sad. Jim retrieved the mangled cart and sold it for scrap. The anniversary cake was a total loss.

KIDS: Experiment at home! Put a blindfold and earmuffs on your dog/cat /hamster/little sister or brother/senile grandparent, and let them loose! On second thought, don't. No — REALLY. Don't. I have to be really clear on this point. All my editors stopped me here and said something about liability, because some people not only don't have a sense of humour, they don't even know what a sense of humour is anymore! (How horribly sad!) *So, of all the things I've said in this book, this is the one I need to be the clearest on: DO NOT RELEASE YOUR SENSORY-DEPRIVED LOVED ONE/NOT SO LOVED ONE/ANIMAL/MATT DAMON/OTHER PERSON INTO THE STREETS...WITHOUT ADULT SUPERVISION.*

— *The Management*

Back to Reality:

After the game, the streets of Hanmer surrounding Little Jim's Grocery Store were littered with a veritable smörgåsbord of waste. The birds came down in droves. Jim's bag boys were out and about, picking up merchandise from the mess while they tried not to get shat on. Little Jim walked down one of the streets where the majority of the shoppers had attempted escape. He directed the bag boys not to leave behind anything worth keeping when he noticed Big Jesse picking up an oozing box of eggs. "Hey!" Jim shouted. "See if any of those eggs are still intact!"

Jesse opened the carton and called back, "Nine of them are smashed, Uncle Jim! See? It's all dripping out and gross!" He held the runny carton up higher for emphasis.

The boss sharply shook his head. "That means three are still good! Separate them and wash them off! Stack 'em good eggs, boy!" Little Jim picked up a badly dented can of baby corn. He chucked it towards a flock of gulls, busily fighting over a rotisserie chicken. The can hit one of them squarely, killing it. The rest of the seagulls took flight, abandoning both dead birds.

Filthy, flying rats, Jim thought to himself.

-7-

U sing some of the profit from the first game, Jim erected a tower. It was cylindrical, spouting out of the building near the front of the store, rising a hundred metres in the air. With a five-metre diameter, it was just large enough to accommodate a simple set of steel stairs circling the inside to the top, and a small elevator shaft up the middle. At the ground level, the tower's elevator opened near the courtesy desk. At the top, it opened to a private suite with a balcony. The suite jutted outwards a dozen metres from the tower, overhanging the store's main entrance.

There were eight-foot-tall, bright red letters painted on the front and back of the tower, like so:

L

I

T

T

L

E

JIM'S

The tower had its own bathroom, concession stand, bar, and balcony seating for a dozen. As the season progressed, Little Jim made a habit of going up there alone for home games, carrying a 20-gauge shotgun and several boxes of birdshot. He'd down a full cart's worth of seagulls in a single game. He considered it a public service.

Jim also used some of the profits to replace all the cash stations in the store with self-checkout terminals. He kept Loretta on to "supervise the system" and fired the rest of the cashiers. Now, you might want to feel badly for Loretta, because she had the unenviable task of sucking Little Jim's cock on demand. But you should know: Loretta wasn't super sharp, and she'd spent her youth walking the streets of downtown Sudbury, spreading her legs and lips for a lot less than she was making now. Jim treated her far better than any John or pimp ever had.

Her new role as supervisor consisted of walking over to customers when they had issues with the system processing an item. Since she never learned to use said system, her solution was always the same: she'd shrug and say, "I guess it's free." Then she'd snap a picture of the barcode, send it to Tom, and let him deal with it.

Well, I'll let *you* decide what to think about Loretta, because we're (mostly) all human, and nobody should throw stones in a glass house. This of course begs the question of why we're letting people into glass houses with rocks in their pockets. The glass house people really need better security screening. Cavity searches seem in order.

Little Jim bought the Hares a used, bright yellow '86 International Blue Bird school bus for away games. With Hanmer being in the middle of nowhere, and Canada being ridiculously big and empty, this meant extremely long drives. Jim figured his bag boys would be plenty keen on tackling people after being cooped up for days in the bus with no air conditioning.

For their first away game, Coach Pecante took the wheel. Like many old geezers, he couldn't drive worth crap, but damned if he'd let anyone else get behind the wheel as long as he was in the vehicle.

Twenty-five Hares settled in for the week-long ride to Port McNeill, British Columbia. The boys were loud and obnoxious, getting on Coach Pecante's nerves before they'd even reached the Trans-Canada Highway. He stopped the bus, stood up, and faced the team. You'd think that stopping a vehicle, getting up, and turning around would have gotten everyone's attention. But you'd be wrong, because people can be pretty dense, and a bunch of football-players-turned-bag-boys were about as thick as they came. Their conversations continued uninterrupted.

Coach Pecante shouted, "HEY!"

When no one looked up, he took his whistle and blew it full bore. It shrieked, echoing inside of the bus. Everyone, save Coach Pecante, instantly covered their ears. "That's better! I can't drive with you idiots screaming! If I hear one more peep out of anyone... just ONE WORD, mind you, I will stop this bus and take away EVERY LAST ONE of your devices! So, put your earphones in and keep yourselves busy!"

They got underway again. Five minutes later, one of the bag boys leaned over to show another the screen of his cell phone. "Look at this!"

The coach stomped on the brakes, slamming everyone's knees into the seats in front of them. He got up and walked down the aisle, collecting all the cell phones, stuffing them in his overburdened fanny pack after relieving it of a tube of BENGAY and a giant green apple. "No talking!"

He'd just pulled the bus back on the road when Brian, who'd been the quarterback on Big Jesse's high school team, muttered, "This is bullshit, yo."

"Excuse me!?" yelled Coach Pecante. He brought the bus to a screeching halt. Once again, knees were bruised. He rooted through his fanny pack. "This phone's yours, right Brian? This one?" He held it up for all to see. "The one with no case, and a busted screen? Ever wonder why you have a busted screen, Brian?"

"Uhh," Brian uttered.

The coach menacingly waved the phone around, opened the door and stepped off the bus onto the paved shoulder.

Brian chased after him. "Hey! Gimmie my phone back!"

"You want your fucking phone? Fetch!" Coach Pecante hurled the phone over the bus and across the road, towards a rock-cut.

Brian instantly gave chase, dashing around the front of the bus, looking neither way, let alone both, as he stepped onto the road. A transport truck going seventeen kilometres per hour over the speed limit hit him full on. For a split second, like a golf ball off the club head, he was flying faster than the truck.

Unlike a golf ball, he had precious little aerodynamic appeal, particularly after the collision. He quickly decelerated, getting hit a second time. The transport truck kept going.

The coach looked up and down the road while the truck sped off. It was otherwise deserted. He opened the cargo hatch along the side of the bus, and hoisted Brian's lifeless body up into it. Then he closed the hatch and got back aboard.

All the boys had witnessed the entirety of the event.

They were all staring at him.

Coach Pecante mulled over his situation for a moment, then unzipped his fanny pack. "Who wants their phone back?"

In unison, the entire team replied, "Me!"

"What's the rule?"

Some of the boys were hesitant to answer. One of them quietly suggested, "No talking?"

Coach Pecante nodded. "Good boys. No talking. And if there's *never any talking*," he added, "everything will be *just fine*."

Twenty-four bag boys continued down the highway.

As for Brian, he was quickly forgotten, because young people have learned to be very adaptable and receptive to change, having attention spans of about eight minutes. Thus, it should come as no surprise that about eight minutes later, someone talked again. This time, Coach Pecante stopped the bus and made the team push it for an hour beneath the blazing sun. This would turn out to be a better deterrent to stop their infernal chatter, as it affected them each individually, whereas watching Brian's gruesome death through the bus windows had made no more impression on them than the infinite grotesque atrocities they'd witnessed on screens throughout their lives. The team spent the rest of the ride in a deep funk, their will to speak squelched by their crumbling, chapped, sunburnt lips. Every patch of exposed skin behind the driver's "do not disturb" line was broiled to perfection. Every set of eyes stared daggers into the coach's back.

Big Jesse got texts by the dozen as the other bag boys bombarded him with complaints. From Kyle to Big Jesse: *WTF!? Your uncle is a sicko. Making us go by bus?? Not worth min wage bro. Wtf.* From Hektor to The Team: *Waz sum1 sittin next to me? Who's Doritos are these? Fuck y'all. Mine now.* From Luke to Big Jesse: *Call your uncle or something!* From Gord to the Team: *Did any of you see the video of that guy getting creamed by a transport? It was amazing but I can't find the link now...*

Big Jesse to the team: *Stop textn me! Nothn I can do. Who u think put us on this shitty bus?* After sending that, Jesse put on his ginormous, noise-cancelling, bass-whoomphing headphones, and zoned out while the bus zoomed by a burnt-out farmhouse on the side of the highway.

Horatio said, "Those headphones may help you ignore things, but the problem isn't going away... I wish it were."

Jesse didn't hear him. He just stared out the window at the passing scenery.

By the time they got to Vancouver Island, they were well behind schedule. "Damn ferry!" Coach Pecante decried. "Damn traffic!" From the ferry onward, the Blue Bird flew north. He drove maniacally, skidding the big yellow bus around even the gentlest of corners, putting the old girl (and the balding tires) to the test. When he saw they were getting close to Port McNeill, he ordered the team to get changed into their uniforms. A couple of passing drivers honked their gratitude for the free show as the boys stripped down. When they reached the store, the coach could see that nearly all of the shoppers had already taken places along the perimeter of the property.

"Jesus, mother...we're late!" He floored it onto the lot, scattering shoppers and spectators. The bus came to a screeching halt a dozen feet from the main entrance. He swung open the door, frantically shouting, "GO, GO, GO! GET INSIDE AND FIND EXIT POINTS! MOVE!"

The coach ran down the stairs, off the bus, and into the store.

The crowd chanted, "Fifty-Nine, Fifty-Eight..."

He found the nearest employee, wildly grabbed the young woman by the shoulders, and screamed, "Where's my battle room!?"

She pointed, blank-faced, to the back of the store.

When he found the room, the screens were all blank. The system wasn't even booted up. "System on!" he commanded. The drone feed monitor screens slowly flared to life, surrounding him. The stats display came on last. Surrounded by information, he donned his headset.

The match began. Bag boys vacated the store, going after shoppers who were quickly scurrying away in all directions. At this venue, there were seven end zones.

Coach Pecante quickly assessed the situation. Assets were rolling away, and it was his duty to stop them. On one monitor, a bird's-eye view was overlaid with translucent red and blue dots representing each team's bag boys, and green dots representing the shoppers. The brighter the shade of green, the higher the value of the cart's contents.

"Standard epsilon formation! There's a high-priority cluster moving east. Fourteen, seven, thirty-three, run hard!"

One of the roads away from the store led up a steady, steep hill. Two of the opposing bag boys were chugging up it, gaining ground on more than a dozen shoppers. Coach Pecante tapped the bright green dots of the three shoppers furthest along, bringing up their cart manifests. Their merchandise combined for just over 9% of total sales.

"Jesse! Swing back around and head up that hill! Take sixty-six and nineteen with you. Run like hell, boy! The three carts at the top are full of electronics!"

Jesse stomped up the hill, passing both of the home team's bag boys.

"Jesse, concentrate on the ones on the top! Sixty-six, nineteen, you slow slobs, get up there! Ignore the clown and the beer bottle, they're worthless. Otherwise, take down the first cart you can. Move it, Jesse! We need this! They're getting away!"

Jesse threaded his way between all the other shoppers. He noticed how nice and smooth the roads were compared to Hanmer's.

Coach Pecante looked at the score. Down by more than 12%, things looked bleak. All the other routes had concluded play.

Jesse caught the farmer in the lead, tackling the large man less than five metres from the end zone. The farmer came down hard on his knees but refused to relent. He turned and began wrestling with Jesse. During their brief scuffle, the untipped cart began rolling backwards. Jesse grabbed the farmer and tossed him aside, but the cart was already out of his reach, and picking up momentum.

The next shopper down the hill, a man dressed as a giant mouse, was still forty metres away from where Jesse stood. The mouse stayed well clear of the downward path of the rogue cart. He was keeping an eye on Jesse, trying to figure out how the hell he was going to get around him. The mouse scurried slower, letting the woman dressed as a Ghostbuster behind him catch up. He sidled up tight to the proton-accelerator-clad competitor, figuring it would give him a fifty-fifty chance of reaching the finish when Jesse had to choose between them.

Oh, the plans of mice and men.

With their focus on one another and on Jesse, neither the Ghostbuster nor mouse noticed when the incoming cart clipped a pebble, deflecting its course towards them. They dove out of the way just as the three carts collided in an explosion of consumerism.

That's when all hell *really* broke loose. Brand new cell phones, tablets, video games and gaming consoles became obstacles tumbling down the hill. In a random conflux, a divergence, a miracle of luck and physics, this domino effect continued as goods and carts tumbled and rolled down, causing every cart to tip in an avalanche of bodies, twisted steel, and merchandise. Jesse stood at the very top of the hill, watching it unfold. As competitors were knocked out of the game, the official scorekeeper tallied the recovered merchandise for the Hares.

-8-

J esse's feat, dubbed "The Hilltop Miracle," would become one of the sport's most replayed moments of all time. It was a bizarre and wonderful phenomenon, but the owner of the store in Port McNeill felt that his team had been fucked out of a win. He quickly contested the result. Jim immediately and retroactively added a rule to the book:

> 15. Should a cart tip as a consequence of a previous cart's tipping, the bag boy credited with tipping the first cart shall be credited with all recovered merchandise within the chain of events.

This would come to be known as "the butterfly effect" rule.

The owner in Port McNeill was furious. But even though Jim just fed him a pile of shit, the owner kept his mouth shut and ate it, lest his team be cast from the profitable, exciting new league.

Coach Pecante, never shy in front of the camera, wasn't afraid to take credit for the victory during his post-game press conference. Fans enjoyed his quirky, memorable quotes, like: "When the bronco bucks, you gotta buck back," or, "If the beer bottle's half full, you haven't drunk enough beer yet," or, "Even when they tear your ticket, you're still holding on to the stub."

When one of the reporters asked the coach, "Coach Pecante, do you use these Yogisms because you're a Yogi Berra fan?" the coach promptly replied, "What the hell does an old cartoon have to do with anything?"

The first season was short. With only four teams, Jim scheduled a twelve-game season with each team playing each other team four times. Playoffs were a simple four-seed bracket set-up. First place from the regular season played last place, while the two middle teams played one another. The winners of those two games played for the honour of being the first Cart Massacre Champions.

The Hares won every game of the regular season. They played the fourth seed Mid-Albertan Strong to open the playoffs, dispatching them easily. In the other semi-final match, the Prairie Pricklers came into Vancouver Island as heavy underdogs to the Piercers, but the Pricklers pulled off a spectacular upset, ending the VIP's season.

With home-field advantage for the championship game, Hanmer was filled to capacity. The roads were clogged, restaurants were packed, and people with spare rooms let them out, filling them with visitors from afar. While the rest of town enjoyed the drippings, Jim sat back and watched money pour into his bank accounts. The championship game was a true Northern Ontarian classic, coinciding with an unseasonably early, heavy, wet snowfall.

From a small booth on the rooftop, two announcers called the action for the livestream: a young, pretty brunette and a heavy-set older man with white hair. The older man turned to the girl, pointedly stating, "Well, Gerry, we're less than fifteen minutes from the bag boys being released, and let me tell you, the shoppers at the perimeter look nervous. See, although it's snowing, the ground is still fairly warm. The snow that fell earlier has turned into a thick, greasy slush, but now it's being hidden by the fresh snow on top. It's treacherous out there.

Better put the winter tires on the carts!"

"You bet, Harve!" Gerry smiled her bleached teeth brightly for the cameras. "Big Jesse comes into this game with a teedee-peegee of just over 4.14, blowing away his competition by a wide margin. And his vo-grr? It's outta this world!"

Harvey nodded. "You're absolutely right, Gerry. And if you're joining us for the first time at home, allow me to welcome you on behalf of Gerry, myself, and the entire team here at the Cart Massacre Network, all the way up to Commissioner McGee. As Gerry was saying, Big Jesse's teedee-peegee, or take-downs per game, means that over the course of the season, he's tipped an average of 4.14 carts per game. But let's not forget the Hilltop Miracle, which skewed that statistic a little. He was awarded eleven take-downs that game, through the butterfly effect ruling. And his vo-grr, or value of goods recovered, is heavily a product of Coach Pecante utilizing him to chase down priority targets."

Gerry tapped a pencil on the table. "True enough, Harve, but there's three other teams out there, and each coach utilized a handful of players more than others to go after those high-valued carts. But no one has a vo-grr like Big Jesse."

"Right you are, Gerry," Harvey conceded. "And now, let's take you back down to some of the antics in the store!"

The stream feed switched to footage of the last few costumed shoppers madly dashing up and down the aisles.

Meanwhile, Jesse sat on an upside-down milk crate near an emergency exit in the stockroom, waiting for the game to start with his snowshoes strapped on. Running on pavement really wasn't their intended purpose. It beat slipping, but it was hell on both the snowshoes and his knees. The modern snowshoes' steel spikes were ground down to rounded nubs from all the days of chasing down shoppers the previous winter. Real shoppers. Not these fake ones dressed like idiots.

"Pecante to BJ — Big Jesse, tune in. Headset on? Good to go?"

Big Jesse sighed. "Yeah. I'm here. Good to go."

"All hands, we're on in five minutes — I repeat, T-minus five minutes. This is it, boys. It's been a hell of a season, and it's been a true honour. It's at times like this I'm reminded of an old saying: Once in a while, you get a chance to do something great. So, do it. Because if you don't, you didn't."

Jesse turned his headset off. "I don't like my job anymore."

Horatio said, "I know that. So why are you still doing it?"

Jesse sat there.

"You're kinda famous now, you know. You seem to be famous everywhere."

Jesse shivered. "I hate being alone."

"You're not alone."

A few minutes later, Jesse burst out the door, scraping his way along the pavement. Running in snowshoes was no easy task. It required all of Jesse's balance, and steadfast legs. He clanked along, sending slush flying. The rest of the bag boys weren't faring as well. Jesse trudged past them while they slipped around, doing their best to stay upright.

One of his sprinting teammates planted a foot and began skidding. Rather than embrace the fall that was clearly coming, he wound up with three limbs high in the air, foolishly trying to regain his balance. He broke two of those limbs when he came crashing down.

Coach Pecante screamed over the comm lines. "Godamnnit! What the hell is going on out there? Haven't you idiots ever driven in the snow before? Slow it down boys! Better a turtle on its feet than a Hare on its ass! And you call yourself Canucks!?"

Bag boys from both teams went at a light jog, barely keeping pace with the shoppers ahead of them, who weren't having much of a better time. Trying to shove the carts through the slush wasn't easy. It clung to the wheels and undercarriage, slogging them down.

Jesse caught up to the closest shopper and began tipping carts over as he passed them. He didn't have time to tackle people. He had to stay on his feet, tipping one cart after another. Clump, clump, clump, tip; clump, clump, clump, tip. He stomped along, tipping cart after cart, leaving dismayed shoppers and spilled groceries in his wake.

A few shoppers accidentally tipped their own carts, ramming them into potholes that had vanished beneath the carpet of snow.

Coach Pecante yelled into Jesse's ear, "Touch those tipped carts, Jesse, touch the carts!"

He'd clomp by, bending over just enough to graze the cart with his fingertips, and keep going. On he went, until he came to the end zone. He turned around and kept on going, catching the odd shopper that had been outside his initial, optimal path.

When he neared the store, he saw the carnage of wet bag boys and shoppers cluttering the first hundred yards of play. The bag boys were already sifting through the recovered goods, picking out anything worth returning to inventory. Jesse looked down the road in the opposite direction. He saw carts in the distance, still well short of the end zone. "Why aren't you guys chasing?"

"Fuck that," Hektor said. "It's a rout, Jesse! You did it! The game's over. Let's get this shit cleaned up and go celebrate."

Jesse turned and sprinted down the road, snowshoes clacking, ripping through slush and snow, closing the gap on the remaining carts in play. He tipped the first one at the 365-

metre marker, and the second just past the 410. There was one small grouping of carts left: six shoppers hustling for the finish within close proximity of one another. Jesse laid out, putting his legs high in the air with each leap, bashing the snowshoes against the ground, chewing up pavement with every stride.

WHAM, WHAM, WHAM, WHAM, WHAM, WHAM.

The shoppers heard him coming. Something odd began happening. Five of the six contestants drifted back together into a tight cluster and began running faster. Those five shoppers sacrificed a rock — a slower woman in a donkey suit. They left her between themselves and Jesse like a guard protecting the zone in the final end of a tight curling match. Her only crime was having shorter legs than the others. A metre short of the 455 marker, Jesse caught the donkey, literally tossing her aside. He took her cart and kept pushing, heaving it forward, bowling it through the remaining five shoppers in a spectacular crush of steel and skeletons.

Luckily, nobody died. Unluckily, nobody walked away except Jesse. He carefully laid a finger on each of their carts in turn, claiming the recoveries. The crowd in the end zone wasn't sure how to react. The fans at home, safely separated by screens, were somewhat less contained. They cheered loudly throughout the world.

In the broadcast booth, Gerry and Harvey found themselves a little lost for words. Harvey eventually spoke first. "Well...I don't think the rules cover any of this. I'm really not sure what to say."

Gerry looked the rules over. "I don't see anything here to say you can't do what he did."

"Snowshoes?"

"Not in the rulebook. Nothing in here to say a player can't

wear snowshoes."

"But no one's ever done it before."

"It's never snowed before during an official match. I mean, snowshoes *are* on their logo for a reason."

"Well, I think it's an unwritten rule that you can't just take a cart and use it as a battering ram against the other shoppers."

Gerry shrugged. "There's no such thing as unwritten rules. In early forms of baseball, you could get the runner out by throwing the ball at him and hitting him with it. They probably did that until some kid lost an eye or went lame from a nasty concussion, then they made new rules. That's why baseball has two-hundred pages worth of 'em."

"Okay, what about those downed carts he touched as he went by? Those three shoppers all tipped their own carts before he'd even gotten there. Do those count?"

"Rule eleven: The contents of a shopper's cart are deemed recovered after a bag boy has disrupted the cart and/or shopper, and the cart is tipped."

Harvey nodded. "Okay, so let's break that down. 'Deemed recovered after a bag boy has disrupted the cart and/or shopper, and the cart is tipped.' The carts were already tipped, then Jesse touched them. So, I don't think the rule applies. Those three carts shouldn't count."

Gerry wasn't so sure. "I don't know, Harve. It just says, 'and the cart is tipped'. It doesn't mention if it has to be tipped before or after the bag boy disrupts it."

"Well, there you go!" Harvey pointed out. "He never disrupted the carts!"

"Sure, he did! He touched them!"

"I don't think a 'touch' counts as a 'disruption', Gerry."

"Well, Harvey, I think a quantum physicist might disagree

with you on the matter."

This precipitated a brief, awkward, very on-air silence between them.

Harvey coughed. "Let's return to the last five carts, hmm? I think we can safely slot this under the butterfly effect rule, but what about using another cart as a plow? Is that legal?"

Gerry shrugged, smugly. "It's not against the rules."

"This obviously isn't what the rules intended."

"But it's not against them."

"A whole season went by, and no one else did it!"

"Maybe that was their loss. It's *not*," she emphasized, "*against the rules.*"

Harvey cringed. "Well, folks, regardless, it was a decisive victory on behalf of the Hanmer Hares. Big Jesse definitely earned the win for his team, on what I think we can safely say was the most entertaining game of the season."

Gerry chimed in, "Sure was Harve, I think you've said it all. So, on behalf of TCMN, Harvey Beckensol, and myself, Gerry Penalta, thank you for tuning in all season long, and we look forward to seeing you again next summer!"

Back in the locker room, Jesse sat by himself. The rest of the team was already out celebrating.

"Quite a game," Horatio said.

Jesse looked at his phone. He checked his bank account. It was in overdraft again. "I can't live like this."

"I wish you'd find something else to do. They wouldn't pay you any less and they couldn't possibly treat you any worse."

Jesse shrugged. He stood up, grabbed his gear, and left Horatio behind.

-9-

Little Jim proudly placed the 2022 Dented Cart Trophy in the storefront window. It featured a tiny, solid nickel, dented grocery cart being pushed by a thin golden woman being tackled by a hefty golden bag boy. Bolstered by the success of the first season, Jim accepted bids from four other store owners, bringing their teams into the league:

The Greybull Greybulls, out of Greybull, Wyoming, USA.
The Thrashers, out of Pleasant Valley, Washington, USA.
The Iron Mountain Men, out of Iron Mountain, Michigan, USA.
The Never-Ending Nightmare, out of Chalk River, Ontario, Canada.

To prevent the teams from becoming too professionalized, Jim and the other owners kept a gentlemen's agreement, stipulating that all bag boys had to be former high school jock washouts, local to the vicinity of the team. If they'd spent any time abroad, they were automatically disqualified from playing. This proved easy for the owners, since that's who they'd been hiring as bag boys in the first place. Jim added five new rules prior to the start of the second season. Some were made after consideration of the first season's championship game, and some were made as concessions to vocal critics making a big stink about health and safety. The media coverage of shoppers clogging hospitals wasn't making for great public relations, anyway.

The five new rules were:

16. Shoppers must wear helmets, knee pads, and elbow pads. Additional safety equipment, such as, but not necessarily limited to the following, are optional: mouth guards, jockstraps, football and/or hockey pads, bear survival suits, etc.
17. Shoppers must pass a general physical exam and be game-certified by a league-appointed doctor.
18. Bag boy footwear must be pre-approved by the league.
19. Bag boys may not purposely handle shoppers' carts or merchandise to facilitate the tipping of additional carts.
20. The League Championship Game shall always be held at Little Jim's Grocery Store in Hanmer, Ontario.

The other seven team owners had a collective beef with rule 20 but ate Jim's shit since they really didn't have any other choice in the matter.

During the off-season, the SPCA and the Greater City of Sudbury regional police forbade Little Jim from shooting down any more birds during the games. Jim simply ignored the writ, paying a stiff fine for each bird he downed. To him, the birds were nothing but flying vermin that interfered with his drones. He just wished he could write the fines off as a charitable donation expense against his business. (Years later, he started claiming it that way, just for the hell of it. He figured that if he got caught, he'd just have to pay the Canada Revenue Agency what he'd rightfully owed them in the first place, plus a little interest, and that if he *didn't* get caught, he'd save reams of money. It was like gambling without a stake, which wasn't gambling at all — it was taking the house for a fucking ride. I won't tell you whether he ever got caught in his gambit, because it's ultimately irrelevant, and what's between a tax dodger and his accountant is entirely sacred.)

For Big Jesse, the off-season meant a return to his routine. Little Jim laid off the rest of the team until spring training, trusting Jesse and his snowshoes to handle things during the winter. Jesse bagged groceries, retrieved carts, and tackled shoppers. But it didn't feel the same. When he slept, his dreams were a mix of confusion and discontent. Horatio visited him there often, speaking to him in hushed tones.

"It wasn't your fault, Jesse," he'd say.

"Yes, it was," Jesse would reply.

Sometimes, Brian would stand beside Horatio, and say, "My death wasn't your fault, either, Jesse."

"Who the hell are you?" Jesse would reply.

The stranger would sadly walk away, leaving Jesse alone with Horatio. They'd spend time together like they used to. Those unconscious moments were happy ones for Jesse. It's such a shame that dreams are fleeting, at best.

Nothing much changed for the other employees at the store. They had no stake in any of the fortune befalling their boss. They continued getting treated like dirt and continued being okay with that. Such was their lot.

Loretta's talents were needed less and less by Little Jim, who was extraordinarily busy with league business. Consequently, her neck problems finally subsided, and she enjoyed a better quality of life for it. Otherwise, her job stayed much the same. She continued to tell customers to take an item if it wouldn't scan. She refilled the plastic bags at each self-checkout station and wiped the surfaces down with disinfectant once a week or so. It was a pretty good gig, all told.

As for Mrs. Tannenbaum? After prolonged mediation with her daughters, Jim settled out of court with her estate, providing generously for her ongoing care, and for the daughters' anguish. Little Jim would often visit Mrs. Tannenbaum, who lay comatose in the hospital. He'd use the room as a confessional. "No one understands me," he'd tell her. "Everything I do is for the right reasons. Why can't people see that?"

She was a very good listener.

On the Flip Side:

In the coin-flip universe, Horatio walked past Little Jim's Grocery Store on his way to the library. He stared at the building, remembering the time he dropped off an unanswered resume. He was thinking of going back to school. He dreaded taking on more debt, but what choice did he have? That grocery store was rather plain-looking. It lacked the tower, bleachers, drone bays, concession stands, battle rooms, and all the other interesting things that had been erected in our little patch of the multiverse.

But that universe did have Horatio. And that was a wonderful thing.

Back to Reality.

-10-

A few weeks into the second season, Little Jim sat by Mrs. Tannenbaum's bedside, looking at her intently.

She lay with her eyes closed, and a sour expression on her face.

"I'd be sour, too, I guess," he said. He glanced at the electroencephalograph screen, which showed continuing low levels of brain activity. "You can die anytime now, by the way." He made a sour face to match hers. "We won our first three games of the season, you know."

A fly landed on her cheek. Her cheek twitched. The fly took off, hiding behind the curtains, where it bounced against the glass pane a few times before settling.

Mrs. Tannenbaum's twin daughters were both elderly as well, and not in nearly as good shape as their mother. They were also in the hospital, slowly dying of lung cancer from lifetimes of inhaling one another's second-hand spinster smoke. Jim went to see them in the extended-care ward after his visit with their mother. He'd visited with them before. They were about as good conversationalists as the elder Tannenbaum. The sisters each looked half dead, which is to say there was at least one dead person between them already.

"Ladies," he said.

One of them started coughing, unable to stop long enough to speak.

The other managed to croak, "We have to *pay* for our

subscription to TCMN." before she, too, began coughing violently. She covered her mouth with a wad of tissues from a box at her bedside. When she finished her fit, the tissues were saturated with blood.

Jim tried to ignore the tissues; fearful she might ask him to dispose of them. "I didn't know you were fans," he said. "I'll take care of your subscription from now on."

At that moment, the Thin Woman, who'd been in the hospital since Jesse crippled her, passed by the room in a wheelchair. After nearly a year of taxpayer-funded physiotherapy, she'd relearned to use her hands well enough to control the chair, and had taken to roaming the halls. When she saw Little Jim, she began mumbling loudly. She said, "You bastard, you did this to me, and now you're making a fortune because of it!"

However, what Jim heard more closely resembled: "Mfmfmmfm Mmmfmfm Mmmfmfmm," because the Thin Woman hadn't quite figured out how to talk again since having her jaw reassembled and half-severed tongue reattached.

Little Jim looked down at the disfigured woman in the wheelchair. He had no idea who she was. She reminded him a little of his childhood friend, Julian. "Hello, there," he said. "Are we having a nice stroll today?"

"MMMMFFFMMM!!!"

"Good," he replied. He smiled dumbly at the beast as one does at a strange dog that they aren't yet sure is friend or foe.

She continued on her way down the hall, mmfmming the entire way.

Jim turned back to the Tannenbaum sisters. "I could get used to it here," he mused. "It's so peaceful."

On his way out of the hospital, Jim glanced in any room with an open door because he was nosy, a bit depraved, and felt a little better about his own life whenever he saw someone in worse shape. "So much needless suffering," he lamented.

One of the rooms he glanced into contained two shoppers that had been severely injured during the championship game. Jim didn't know this, nor would he care too much if he had, since they'd signed waivers exonerating him of any liability when they participated. He walked past all the hand sanitizer stations in the lobby, using none, then out the sliding glass doors. It's not that Jim didn't respect the need to sanitize his hands after touching things in a hospital, because he did. Jim didn't sanitize because he recognized that hospitals are disgusting, filthy places to begin with, and he'd been entirely conscious of not touching anything during his visit. Outside the hospital, he squinted his eyes in the sunshine. It was a beautiful day with nary a cloud in the sky.

He drove back to Hanmer in his Tesla Model S, pulling into the store parking lot just after noon. He didn't really feel like going in. He took a stroll down a side street, eventually coming to what he liked to call "The Pizza Place of Many Faces." He called it that because the business had been bought and sold more than a dozen times in the past decade, each new owner re-branding and opening what would surely be the best, most successful pizza place in town, despite every former owner's inability to do the same. The building looked pristine. The newest owner had put more effort into it than any of the previous ones had. The siding, roof, and windows were brand new, the parking lot freshly paved. The neon "open" sign was dark. Jim frowned and looked at his watch.

The canopy over the entrance sported the name of the establishment: Pizza Pi. Underneath, smaller letters read, "Home of the quarter third, quarter half, and the full quarter."

Jim walked to the storefront window and peered through. He could see a middle-aged man inside with long, flowing blond hair, blue eyes, and decent physique.

Seeing Little Jim at the window, the man smiled, waving him in.

Jim opened the door. "Your sign's off."

"Yeah, I don't open for a few more minutes. I'm Elvis, owner of Pizza Pi. You might as well turn on the sign, if you don't mind." He pointed at the dangling cord.

"Hmm? Oh. Sure." Jim pulled the cord, and the neon lit up.

"Just give me a couple minutes to pull one of these out of the oven. You looking for a slice, yeah? I've got pep and cheese, deluxe, a Canadian, and an American ready to go."

"American? What's on the American?"

"Dissent and angst. Hah. It's New York–style pepperoni, the regular pepperoni, ham, bacon, sausage, and Canadian bacon."

"Huh. Canadian bacon on the American?"

"Sure, Americans love Canadian bacon. Americans love ham in general, and Canadian bacon is the best ham of all."

"Huh. I think everyone loves ham. Except the ones who don't." Jim shrugged.

Elvis pulled a pepperoni pizza out of the oven and walked it to the counter, where he opened the pizza display case and slid the pie in.

Jim said, "Actually, that looks pretty good. I'll have a slice of that."

"Sure thing. So, what'll it be? A quarter third, a quarter half, or a full quarter?"

Little Jim looked at him quizzically.

"A quarter third is one third of a quarter of this pizza. A quarter half is half of a quarter of this pizza. And a full quarter.

…"

"Is a quarter of a pizza."

"You got it, partner!"

"Huh. I guess I'll have the quarter half."

"Good choice. Drink?" Elvis pointed to the pair of drink dispenser units embedded into the wall, featuring touch screens and nearly infinite flavour combinations.

Jim declined with a wave of the hand. "Don't people find the menu confusing?"

Elvis shrugged. "I don't mind explaining."

"Huh. How long have you been open?"

Elvis sliced a quarter of the pizza out of the pan, sliced it again in half, and put one of the halves on a large paper plate. The tip of the slice draped lazily over the edge of the plate, which was quickly becoming translucent with grease. "This is week seven."

Jim paid with cash. "How's business been, if you don't mind me asking?"

Elvis gave him his change, then took a look at the clock in the dining area. "See for yourself. I officially open in three, two, one…" He pointed across the street to the small local brewery. A loud steam whistle blew, and sixty-five employees in blue jumpsuits walked out, crossing the quiet street to the pizzeria.

Jim took his slice to a corner table and watched the show. What most amused him were the drink machines. He observed one woman order an extra-large Sprite mixed with Cranberry Canada Dry Ginger Ale and a shot of cherry flavouring. She seemed pleased with the concoction, which made sense, since there were more calories in her cup than on her plate. Elvis hustled like a mad man for forty-five minutes to clear the lunch rush. He sold nearly ten of the enormous pizzas in total, a quarter third, quarter half, and full quarter at a time. The crowd quickly thinned to nothing as the brewery employees ate and dashed back to work, leaving Jim and Elvis alone.

Elvis said, "I only make four kinds of pizza. I don't take special requests. You can't order anything but what's on the menu, and a whole pizza costs the same as it would to buy four full quarters, or eight quarter halves, or twelve quarter thirds. Makes my life more manageable. I read somewhere that when McDonald's started, they had nine things on the menu. Nine. Can you believe that?" Elvis snagged the last denomination of pizza from the display. "Hmph. Deluxe," he complained. He picked off the green peppers and ate it anyway.

Jim nodded. "But you're supposed to please the customer. You can't please the customer by only offering one thing."

"Four things," Elvis retorted with his mouth full. "Five, if you include service with a smile. A bajillion, if you include those things," he said, pointing to the drink machines. "I'm a one-man operation. I can only offer so much."

"Huh. Yeah. Those drink dispensers. People seem to really like them."

"I'm surprised the deli take-out of your store doesn't have one."

"Huh? Oh."

Elvis laughed, and crumbs flew out of his mouth. "What, you don't think I'd recognize Little Jim McGee? You're not exactly under the radar anymore, pardon the pun."

Jim frowned. "Huh. No, I guess I'm not."

"Got a minute? I need a break anyway. Come out back with me for a smoke." Elvis crammed the last of the pizza into his mouth and grabbed a sign from under the counter. He stuck it on the front door, informing customers that he'd be back in fifteen minutes. In reality, he'd normally return anywhere from nineteen to thirty-one minutes later. The time varied, depending on how much water he'd consumed, how stressful the lunch rush had been, and how backed up his digestive system was from not getting enough fibre in the days prior. In this case, he'd return forty-four minutes later to serve a young woman who, upon the advice of the sign, had been standing hungrily out front nearly the entire time.

It's okay to let that woman wait, though, since I'm still telling the story of what happens out back between Jim and Elvis, and her narrative doesn't really coincide with theirs.

Elvis led Jim out the back of the pizzeria to a small parking lot. It was surrounded by high fences with a locked gate, allowing entry to the side street. A couple dumpsters took up a full quarter of the lot, while Elvis's Purple El Camino took another quarter. The immediate area by the door was covered by a small canopy jutting out from the building, just large enough to shade a set of bright, multi-coloured, sturdy deck chairs and the beer cooler between them.

"My personal retreat," Elvis said. He sat down in one of the chairs, entreating his guest to do the same in the other.

Jim sat graciously. "This is nice." He meant it.

"It's not quite your tower, but it's a start," said Elvis, pointing to the monstrosity in the distance. He reached under his chair, producing a package of smokes. He pulled a cigarette out and lit up. He offered one to Jim, who politely refused.

"Huh," said Jim. "We all have to begin somewhere. This is as good a place as any. I've seen a dozen places come and go in this spot. You seem to be doing well."

"It's a living." He took a drag of his smoke.

"Who did your renovations?"

"Me. I did everything. I bought the building, spent three months doing all the work, and opened. I had no money to pay other people to fuck it up, anyway. One-hundred-percent Elvis."

"All or nothing, huh?"

"Damn right." He took another long drag from the cigarette, then tapped the ashes into a coffee can on the ground.

Jim got a lungful of dirty air and began coughing.

"Sorry. I take it you don't approve?" Elvis twitched the dart between his fingers. "See, I did the math. I had just enough money left to either buy this shithole and get it going to my liking, or to live in poverty for maybe five more years. I figure my back's got maybe — *maybe* — fifteen more years of work left in it, if I'm lucky. I've already had both knees done. Even the way I'm killing it here, one way or another, the numbers won't add up." He took one last drag, then tossed the cigarette into the coffee can. "So, I took up smoking. Can't afford to live forever. I gotta die by the time I'm sixty-seven, man. Know what I mean?"

"Huh. You're... different."

Elvis laughed and slapped Jim on the shoulder. "Coming from you, I'll take that as a sincere compliment. We eccentrics need to stick together!"

Elvis opened the cooler, which contained 14 bottles of low-carbohydrate beer, 312 cubes of ice in various states of decay, 16,312 millilitres of water, and 49 beer caps. "Gettin' slushy in there," he said. He opened the valve at the bottom, letting the excess water splash out onto the pavement. He took a beer and offered one to Jim.

"Hmm," said Jim. He looked at his watch, then reached down and took a bottle.

They spent the next thirty-eight minutes talking. Once they wrapped up their discussion, Elvis contemplated his package of cigarettes while Jim finished off his beer.

Jim put the empty bottle beside the cooler and stood up. "I'll have my people do up the paperwork. Thanks for the beer."

"Uh-huh," replied Elvis, distantly. He tossed the nearly full pack of smokes into the coffee can of ashes.

Another writer once told me that you should tell your story as it happens. That always seemed silly to me, because although Little Jim and Elvis obviously spent some time discussing things that are relevant to this story, they also spent a great deal of time discussing things that were of no relevance whatsoever. Elvis, in particular, found any excuse to segue into endless rants about things that might have been useful had he been a contestant on "Jeopardy!" but had very little value otherwise.

For instance, at one point during their conversation, Elvis said, "And you know, some birds have the stupidest species names. The people who named them had to have known what they were doing. Like, seriously now. C'mon, man. There's the bufflehead, the bananaquit, the bushtit; there's dickchissels, the American woodcock, and of course, there's my personal favourite, boobies." He took a long swig of beer. "So, Jimmy-boy, would you say you're more of a boobie or a dickchissel kind of guy?" When Jim didn't immediately answer, Elvis slapped his shoulder and laughed. "Ah, don't worry about it, eh? You can like both. Hah!"

So, as a writer, what am I to do? That above passage was a *high* point of the side-tracking. He also talked about the time he had hemorrhoids. Do you really want to hear more about that? How he couldn't sit for a month, and vowed to eat more salad in the future? And how he considered it a moral victory the first time he could shit again without crying? And how when you're desperate for hemorrhoidal cream, it's always hiding on the bottom fucking shelf at the pharmacy? No, I didn't think so.

Anyhow, talk of that sort was inconveniently dispersed through the duration of their chat, and since I haven't the inclination to transcribe the entire conversation, and since I think we can both agree that you wouldn't want to read it all, I'm going to do you the favour of summarizing what transpired between them.

Jim offered to purchase 51% of Pizza Pi for $100,000. In this partnership, Jim agreed to do all the legwork in franchising out the business. Or rather, Jim's people, with Jim's money, would do the legwork to franchise out the business. Elvis would continue working the current location, which would serve as a benchmark for the future expansion stores.

Jim enjoyed the peace of the back lot a moment longer before heading back into Elvis's shop. He returned a moment later. "You've got a customer waiting out front."

"Huh? Oh. Shit. Okay. Thanks. Want to let them in? I'll be right there."

Jim took the sign off the door, tossed it on the nearest table and left, allowing the waiting woman to enter.

Ever seen someone irritated from waiting nearly a half-hour more than they rightfully should have? They're not happy. Know what makes them less happy? When they get inside and find out there's no pizza ready. Know what makes Elvis unhappy? Customers who yell at him. Know what makes everyone happy? Free pizza and drinks, and coupons for more free pizza and drinks, which is what Elvis parted with to mollify the angry woman. She sat at a table and waited while Elvis prepped a pie and rushed it into the oven. By the time she'd eaten and left, Elvis had a dozen more pizzas prepped for the coming dinner rush. He slid the last one onto a tall cart, which he rolled into a chiller. He put the sign back on the door and went out to his little veranda. Relaxing in his chair, he unconsciously reached for his pack of smokes. He grasped air before remembering he'd relocated the pack to the ashes in the coffee can.

"Huh," he grimaced. He sent a text to his buddy Eric: *Long time no see. Let's chill? Like old times. Bring green?* Elvis opened another beer and relaxed. He scratched his balls through his pants. Then he unbuckled his belt and gave his balls a good rub through his underwear while he contemplated that in the course of an afternoon, everything in his life had changed. He also thought about offering Eric a free pizza to entice him to come over faster, or at all. He was just about to send another text, when his phone vibed.

Eric: *Hey. Yeah. Busy as always. Million things on the go. Haven't heard from you in ages. What's changed? Pizza Hut buy your secret recipe for a million bucks? Corpse-play 101, man. If you find a way to live they find a way to make you dead again. Money kills everything. I'm free maybe Sunday. Maybe. Tomorrow I am at parents. Doing chores. U know.*

Elvis: *Now? Free extra large.*

Elvis waited for a reply. He drank some more beer. He only drank ultralight beer because it gave him less gas. Eventually, his phone vibed again.

Eric: *3 extra larges. Whole whole wholes or whatever the fuck you call them. Can only stay a couple hours. Early day tomorrow. Pizza for family. Well 2. Not all. And a calzone. Gonna have to cancel like three meetings to make this happen if its gotta be now.*

Elvis laughed. He replied, *Fucking baby. 2 Pizzas and a big calzone. As if you will eat a big pizza and a calzone all to yourself.*

Eric replied, *DONE. There in 30. Or I'm free. Not really.*

NOTHING is free. All meat calzone. And mushrooms. One pep and one deluxe for pizzas.

Elvis went back into the store. No one was waiting outside this time. He took the sign down, opting to simply close for the night. He put a sign up on the door that read, "Closed for evening due to unforeseen circumstances. Please come again. Apologies." The sign looked nice. Elvis had very fluid, neat handwriting. He pulled two pepperoni pizzas and one deluxe pizza from the chiller. He took one of the pepperoni pizzas, added a grotesque, heart-clogging amount of meat, a pile of mushrooms, some more sauce and cheese on top, then folded the whole thing in half. He fringed the edges, brushed garlic butter over it, and popped it, along with the pizzas, in the oven. He set the timer, then he boxed up the remainder of the pizza he'd cooked for the angry waiting woman and brought it out back for himself. Why did everyone love deluxe?

He contemplated his dreary parking lot. The dumpsters stunk. His car stunk. The ashtray stunk. He picked the stinky green peppers off the pizza, flicking them into the coffee can. He smelled his clothes. They stunk of cigarette smoke and sweat. Not necessarily in that order, particularly around his armpits, groin, and ass. Speaking of his ass, he reached down to give it a healthy scratch, once again using his underwear as a barrier between the filth and his fingers, making sure to get in deep enough to alleviate the itch. This went on for a while until the oven timer began beeping.

He went back inside, took the pizzas out, sliced them, boxed them, and left them on the counter. Then he pulled the calzone from the oven and went back outside, ate a slice of pizza, drank another beer, and swam around in his own headspace for a little while. Maybe things wouldn't have to stink so much anymore.

Nearly an hour later, Eric showed up. Elvis let him in through the back gate. Eric had a disheveled mop of black hair, and a thick, short, roguishly unruly beard. His eyebrows were unruly, too, but in a less fortunate sort of way, springing out in every direction on the cartesian plane. He had the look of a man who knew the world was going to end at any moment. He wore an old black hoodie, black jeans, flashy green sneakers, and a bright orange backpack.

By the time he'd arrived, the cooler was down to 8 bottles of low-carbohydrate beer, 243 cubes of ice in various states of decay, 1,231 millilitres of water, and 53 beer caps. The two unaccounted for beer caps were on the ground near the dumpsters, because although Elvis convinced himself that he could throw them into the dumpster from where he sat, he came up short twice.

Eric sat down in the other chair and grabbed a beer. He twisted off the cap, flinging it with a snap of his fingers clear across the lot into the dumpster. It clattered against the far side of the bin, landing softly on a bag of trash.

Elvis scowled. "You have no idea how many times I've tried to do that. I hate how you make it look so easy."

"All in the wrist, my man. Maybe I jerk off too much. So. What's this about? Pizzas ready? Where's my calzone? I'm starving. You should put those on the menu. Your calzones are wicked good."

"The calzones are too much work and take too long to cook. Your food's inside getting cold. Help yourself."

Eric came back, holding the giant calzone in both hands. It was still warm. He took an enormous bite. "Mmm," he mumbled, sitting down.

"Some shit went down today. Some crazy, crazy shit. I'm not even sure what just happened."

"Well, have another death stick and tell me about it."

"No. I quit. See?" Elvis pointed to the pack of smokes in the ash can.

"What. You just up and quit? There's smokes in that pack?"

Elvis nodded.

"The hell?" Eric set the calzone on his lap and reached down between the chairs. He plucked the pack of smokes from the can, though it was covered in ashes and green peppers. "Aww, wha' the fuck, man?" He shook the pack like a wet dog, as far away from his face as he could. Then he wiped it down on the side of his pants. He opened it up and looked inside. There were still sixteen smokes in it. "Fucking elitist *business owner*. I can get ten bucks for this, *easy*." He crammed the smokes into his bag. "Oh yeah — I brought you something." He pulled a large, stiff, brown leather pouch from his backpack, handing it to Elvis.

Elvis smiled, immediately recognizing the gift. Two years ago, Elvis helped Eric empty out the hoarded house that had belonged to Eric's late uncle, a fanatic bird watcher. The job took three days and hundreds of Hefty bags. The binoculars were the only thing of any value whatsoever in the house, not that they were worth much.

"Thought you'd like them. My mom thought my brother would want them, but he never came to pick them up, so fuck him. She needs room for more shoes, anyway. Freaking elitist. Play with those things later. I know you. You elites want to play with new toys the second you get them. Us common folk are patient. We appreciate things when the time is right."

Elvis sighed. "Eric, the constant hustler. Just because I fill in some paperwork and pay some taxes now doesn't mean I'm not still hustling. I hustle all day. You're more of an elitist than I am. When's the last time you got your hands dirty doing *anything*?"

Eric feigned being hurt by the remark. He clutched his backpack to his chest. "Hey. Take that back. I don't need this elitist abuse."

Elvis laughed. "You're either the realest person I know, or the fakest. Either way, you're a character."

"Uh-huh. So. What's this all about?"

"Later. I need to ease into this. Bring anything special?"

Eric raised an eyebrow. "Alright. I'll play along, *hustler*," he said. "That depends. Is your highness wanting the dopest dope or the wussy weed tonight?"

"For a time like this? I don't suppose you have anything *really* special for us?"

Eric smiled. "Fuckin' Elvis. The things I do for you. I had to cancel shit for this, you know. Move things around and stuff. Okay. Let's see." He dug around the bottom of his backpack until he produced a small, square, rusty tin. He opened it and pulled out a foil wad, unwrapping it to reveal an enormous glowing bud of sparkling wonder. He brought it up to his face and inhaled deeply, then passed it ever so carefully to Elvis for his inspection.

Elvis smelled it briefly, then handed it back. "Nice," he said indifferently.

Eric scowled. "No appreciation. You have no idea how far this has travelled. How many hands it had to pass through, all to get here, right now, for *you*."

"I appreciate what it *does*."

Eric rolled his eyes. He closed the cooler and set his calzone atop it. He produced a small grinder from his backpack and slowly shredded the bud. Then he pulled out a thin hardcover book and some papes, laid the book atop his knees, and used the makeshift table to roll a fat joint.

Elvis asked, "So, how's Mel?"

"Annnd it begins," Eric said. "Like you didn't know? I had to dump her. Couple weeks ago."

"No, man, I didn't know. I'm sorry. I thought things were going well."

"Really? Figured you'd know. You two text more than anyone I know."

Elvis shook his head. "Not since all this, man. You know how it's been. Putting this all together... then running it. There hasn't even been time to breathe. I've been totally off the radar. I'm sorry, man. Really. What happened?"

"She moaned."

"I thought they were allowed to moan once?"

"Only at the end, when I pull out. One little gasp. Maybe once at the beginning too, when I put it in. You know, if she's really tight."

"That's not what this was?"

"No. I was fucking her, and I was having a little trouble getting into the right mindset to get off, and it went on for a while, and then... she just kind of had a little tremor and moaned. It ruined everything. I had to tell her to leave."

"You just... you just kicked her out!? Because she was *enjoying* it?"

"That's not how it works, man. She's *supposed* to enjoy it, but she also has to be perfectly still. That's the whole point. It'll never be the same now."

Elvis shook his head. "I'll never understand you."

"And I hope to hell you never do, either. And what the hell's to understand? You have some seriously messed-up bedroom habits of your own from the sound of it."

"Pleasuring someone to their ultimate satisfaction, no matter the method, is hardly a *seriously messed up habit*," Elvis replied. "Wanting your partner to be a corpse in bed? *That's* messed up."

"The hell is wrong with you tonight? Do you want this herb I brought for you or not? I don't have to take this. I've told you this all before. It's not about wanting to fuck a corpse at all. That's sick. Disgusting. You just don't get me. We all enjoy different things, Elvis. And she *knew*, you know. She knew the moment she moaned that she'd fucked it all up. She knew it'd never be the same. I helped her pack, helped get her set up in her new place. It was amicable."

Elvis shook his head. "Don't get you, man. Don't get you at all, sometimes. When I met her at that party, and she told me she was into that, and I told her I had a friend that was into it, she literally called me a liar to my face. She thought I was shining her on. I can't believe things didn't work out. I can't believe neither of you even texted me to let me know."

Eric gave Elvis a pouty face. "Whassa matta, boo? Not as good a matchmaker as you thought? There'll be another, one day. I'm practically asexual anyway. I'm in no rush." He sparked up the joint and took a haul. "Still enough for one more," he said, before he began coughing violently. "You realize I only smoke this shit with *you*, right? Only Neanderthals still *smoke* it. I had to stop at three stores to find papes on the way here, just for you. God forbid you'd ever use the vaporizer." He took another haul and passed it over.

"Your effort is appreciated." Elvis held the joint up between his fingers, watching it for a moment while it burned.

Eric gave him a cold look. "Hey! Do you fucking mind? You're letting it drift away. I've been saving that for a special occasion, so this better the fuck be it."

Elvis took a long, deep haul. He held it in, and started playing with the binoculars again, giving them a once over. "These are really nice."

"Are you going to fixate on those binoculars for the next hour and then fall asleep?"

"Why, are you hoping I'll pass out and you can go necrophiliac on my ass?"

"You know what? Fuck you! Give me back my binoculars!"

Elvis went into a small coughing fit of hysteria. He looked through the binoculars at Jim's tower while fiddling with the focus. With the high fences of the back lot, Jim's tower was the only thing Elvis could really see with the binoculars, unless he wanted to look closely at the tires of his El Camino. "You want corpse-play, Eric? Finish rolling that next joint. I've got a story for you."

So, Elvis told Eric about his day. The bottles of beer dwindled away until there were only empties. Elvis was sure of this, because he swept his hand through the ice-cold water several times to make sure there wasn't just one more.

Eric, after absorbing Elvis's tall tale, asked, "Little Jim, huh?"

"Little Jim."

"Are you sure that you didn't just hit your head this morning?"

"I'm sure."

"Carbon monoxide leak in the store? You're clearly hallucinating."

"No! It happened!"

Eric looked at him doubtfully.

"I didn't make this up, Eric. This is for real."

"This pizzeria was your dream. You talked about it for years. You just *sold* it?"

"Only 51% of it. And this place wasn't my *dream*. It was just an idea. A good one. A way to keep on going awhile longer."

"This is so *wrong*. You weren't kidding when you said corpse-play. You just laid down and *took it*. What did you agree to?"

Elvis shrugged. "Getting rich," he replied. "I told you years ago — this world is going to be an amazing place for the few who can afford it. How could I say no? Can you imagine what I'll be able to do with the money?"

"You know he fired my mom and my two aunts when he installed those job-killing self-checkout machines, right? I don't know about this. I think you finally had things figured out, and you just derailed. He grew up in this community and he gives nothing back. We're on our last leg, here. Everyone's out of work. Just look at yourself. You run this whole place by yourself. Robot cashier, robot drink dispenser. Robots everywhere doing everything. Something's gotta give. It's all coming down around us."

"I don't know. I'm feeling more optimistic all of a sudden."

"You're giving it up for all the wrong reasons."

Elvis scoffed. "I can't believe you'd think *this* was my dream. To work like a slave in what should be my glory years? I'm tired. My dream was to own a mansion on the beach of some exotic island."

"And bang all the locals?" Eric asked.

Elvis laughed. "Maybe."

"Get all your vaccinations first." Eric picked up the binoculars and peered at Jim's tower. "You're sure about this?"

"He already transferred me the money on good faith. The loan on the building is his problem now. He owns the business."

"This is going to complicate everything."

"Things have always been complicated. You know, if this all pans out, we'll be rich beyond belief."

"If. If it all pans out. And what do you mean, *we*?"

"I'll need my entourage. Someone's going to have to deal with all the locals on my island. You're the most elite hustler I know."

They had a good laugh and smoked the last joint.

Elvis eventually fell asleep in his chair. Eric proactively tossed a sealed bag with an ounce of premium weed onto Elvis's lap, left behind the remaining papers and a lighter, then he stumbled into the shop, plundered the nearly 200 bucks from the till, and took his pizzas. He left through the back gate while Elvis snored.

-11-

The next day, someone knocked on the front door of Pizza Pi. It was nearly noon, and Elvis was still sleeping out on his chair, hungover. He'd been dreaming of having sex with Eric's old girlfriend, Mel. In his dream, someone started jumping up and down on the floor above, rocking the ceiling. The noise threw Elvis off his rhythm, and he woke up.

There's something preciously wonderful about not being able to feel your hangover while you're still unconscious. When Elvis opened his eyes, the sun was high in the sky. The noise of the town surrounded him. He caught a sharp taste of sulphur dioxide in the air. He heard someone banging at the front door. All these sensations were equally excruciating. He checked his phone for the time. Realizing he had less than fifteen minutes before the lunch rush, he panicked. He tried to hurry to his feet, felt an intense wave of nausea, and immediately sat back down. He leaned over his armrest and puked into the cooler.

When he made it to the front door, he opened it to a thin, tall man in a grey pinstriped suit, carrying a briefcase. Elvis let him in, then walked back to the kitchen before the guy could smell him. Elvis yelled, "Just grab yourself a drink if you'd like and take a seat! I'm going to be fifteen minutes, then there'll be some pizzas ready." He remembered the pizzas he'd prepped ahead of time for the dinner rush the previous night, before he'd closed the store. He opened the cooler. They weren't exactly the freshest looking. The dough and most of the toppings had dried out. He tossed a handful of fresh cheese over each pizza and chucked them in the oven for the coming rush.

Then he hit the bathroom to wash up. When Elvis walked back into the kitchen nine minutes later, the oven timer was already beeping. On the bright side, he looked somewhat presentable after a good ball, armpit, and face-washing at the sink. On the not-so-bright side, the pizzas were burning. He rushed them out of the oven, looked them over, shrugged, and filled the displays just as the lunch rush hit. The man in the suit sat in the corner, patiently observing.

The store filled with people, and Elvis served thirteen customers without incident, all of whom paid with credit or debit. The fourteenth customer opted to pay with cash. Elvis punched in the order, took the man's twenty-dollar bill, and opened the till.

Where the fuck was his float? Elvis, stunned, looked accusingly at the man in the suit. The man in the suit looked back at him. The man in the suit didn't know why Elvis looked angry, and he didn't care, either. The man in the suit was having a difficult time making sense of what he was seeing, juxtaposed against what he was carrying in his briefcase.

"Excuse me," Elvis told the customer. "I just have to grab some smaller bills."

Elvis went to the back of the store, where he spent four minutes rooting through his office drawers and wallet, looking for change. He returned to the front. "Sorry, I can't break that," he told the man. He gave the guy his slice of pizza for free.

Well, I'm not going to say all people are assholes, because they're not. Although in this case, Elvis had difficulty convincing himself of that because upon seeing the previous transaction, all the remaining customers in line opted to use cash, too. People who normally ordered half quarters ordered full quarters, and people who normally ordered third quarters ordered half quarters.

The man in the suit smirked.

The ambiance in the pizzeria was different. Quiet. Discontent. Maybe it was the smell of burnt pizza. Maybe it was the wafting scent of misery, hate, and distrust. Elvis ran out of pizza before the last few customers had been served. He gave them vouchers for free pizza on their next visit. They returned to the brewery with empty stomachs, and the memory of an unpleasant experience.

Once Elvis handed out vouchers to the final customer, he approached the man in the corner. "You didn't order."

The man nodded. "I'm Little Jim's attorney. I have some papers for you to sign."

"That was fast."

"Little Jim was anxious to get this done today."

"I see. Come back into the kitchen."

The lawyer followed Elvis, making a point to scrutinize the burned pizza one of the customers was eating. He looked at it the same way he looked at most things, which is to say, contemptuously. He laid his briefcase on the kitchen counter, opened it, took out a thick, neatly bound document, and laid it out. He proceeded to summarize the 102,374 words that legally entitled Elvis to precisely 49% of what he'd created. By the time they were finished, Elvis had signed in 17 places, and initialed in 132 more. The lawyer gathered the papers and left, mentally noting that he'd need to bill Jim for three hours at five-hundred dollars an hour, because he'd actually spent two hours and two minutes in the pizzeria.

Elvis looked around the empty storefront. It was far messier than it usually was after a lunch rush. Fewer people had thrown out their own trash. A drink was carelessly spilled on the floor, with no effort made to clean it. A pool of water remained where some ice had fallen from the drink machine. Elvis looked in the empty register one last time. He closed the store and went home to sleep off his worsening hangover.

He woke up in the late evening, his body yearning for food, water, and a shower. He treated it to beer, beef jerky, a dill pickle, and a face wash, in that order. Then he went to the living room, flopped onto his couch, and put Sportsnet Ontario on television.

Coach Pecante's shiny bald head filled the screen during a post-game media interview. A reporter in the gallery was asking him about their latest victory, which they'd won decisively, recovering 53% of sales to their opponent's 29%. The Coach leaned onto the podium, pulling the microphone close to his face. "We have to really give this one to Big Jesse. There's no two ways about it, and if there were, I'd take the third way." He pointed to another reporter.

The reporter said, "We're four games into the season, and the Hares are unbeaten. Of all the teams in the league, which one worries you the most?"

Coach Pecante looked at the reporter and shrugged. "The Piercers are a good team this year. They're three and one, and eager to square dance." He pointed to another reporter.

That reporter stood up and said, "Your players have been very vocal online about their treatment during road trips. They say that the methods of the Hare franchise are barbaric. They claim that they're forced to sleep on the bus, that the bus has no air conditioning, and that they aren't allowed to talk. Do you have any comment?"

"With our proven track record, if our methods are wrong, then I don't want to be right. This team is a hornet's nest, and each player is a wasp. Sometimes you have to kick the honey hive to get the bees moving. Just like Mohammad Ali. Next question?"

Elvis turned it off. What had he done?

On the Flip Side:

Meanwhile, in the alternate universe, Elvis really found a good rhythm, smoking himself to death while making people fatter a full quarter at a time. It kept him busy. The Thin Woman continued stealing grocery carts uninterrupted, hoarding them in her backyard. Coach Pecante was just Mr. Pecante, a lonely, creepy old man with a good teacher's pension, and lots of time to go hiking and camping by himself. Tom, the assistant manager, was still waiting for Jim to retire so he could buy the store. Loretta continued sucking Little Jim's little dick, though she still had a staff of cashiers to manage. Her neck was constantly sore. Mrs. Tannenbaum was dead, though her husband was very much alive, enjoying the insurance money. He'd just come back from a three-week vacation to Cuba, where he'd indulged in several "happy ending" massages with several Cuban beauties. Old isn't dead after all. Horatio began working on a physics degree at Laurentian University, after taking on a crippling amount of debt to go back to school.

Back to Reality:

A week later, the Hares' fifth game of the season was a home affair against the Mid-Albertan Strong. It rained heavily. Live attendance was light, with a smattering of spectators seated in the rooftop bleachers, and even fewer people down in the parking lot. Elvis received an invitation to join Jim in his private suite.

Upon arrival, Loretta escorted him to the elevator, accompanying him up. She smiled flirtingly. "I'm told that you make a good pizza. You must have strong hands, working that dough all day."

Elvis grinned. "Strong enough. They get the job done."

"I bet." She looked him up and down. "No ring?"

Elvis laughed. "Once before. Never again." He blatantly looked at her left hand. "You neither?"

"Mmm, nope. No man's tied me down yet... at least not tightly enough to keep me from escaping."

The elevator reached the top and dinged. The doors swept open. Loretta motioned to the balcony. "Little Jim is already waiting for you."

A chagrined Elvis walked off the elevator. He winked at Loretta as the doors closed, then he went to sit beside Little Jim.

Jim was busily looking around, gun in hand. The seagulls were laying low for the moment, though that would change once the game began. All the home games thus far had been bright affairs for Jim, with the gulls out in force.

Elvis regarded the sight below them. Shoppers were just beginning to exit the store, making their way to the starting line at the edge of the property. "This is quite the thing you've created. You must be very proud."

Jim shrugged. "I prefer baseball."

"Huh." Elvis looked towards his pizzeria in the distance.

Jim put his gun down for a moment. "We've installed a Pizza Pi kiosk in my store. All the other stores in the league, too. Take-out and delivery at each location."

Elvis nodded, since he'd already resolved himself to having no choice in outcomes anymore. "You've installed brick ovens? Flavour won't be the same otherwise."

"Oh, no, that's not cost efficient *at all*. We put in electric conveyor belt ovens. Raw pizza in one end, cooked pizza out the other."

"Ah," Elvis said. What Elvis was actually thinking, though, was that those belt-driven ovens didn't turn out a pizza that tasted anything like one out of a traditional brick oven.

"Oh, and we changed up some of the ingredients. We were able to get a much better bulk price on different brands of sauce, cheese and pepperoni, et cetera."

"Ah," Elvis replied. He stared down at the parking lot disinterestedly.

"We created a logo, too." Little Jim grabbed his phone and brought up a picture of it to show Elvis.

They'd added a giant, flourished exclamation point after the name, changing the franchise from Pizza Pi to Pizza Pi! The logo itself was a picture of Elvis from the waist up, smiling toothily, wearing nothing but a white apron with the name "Energetic Elvis!" printed on it, and a pale blue ball cap. The ball cap had the exact same logo on it, creating an infinite loop of half-naked Elvises smiling like a big goofy fuckwad.

Elvis jumped out of his chair. "WHAT THE HELL IS THIS!?" He stood, leering over Little Jim. "WHAT... THE... FUCK!?"

Little Jim just grinned. "What? It tested great with the six-to-twelve demographic. You'll be a hero. And rich. Besides, it's too late. Part of this game's local promo is the Energetic Elvis special offer. If the Hares win, you get a free large pizza with every order. All the different locations are running the same deal for their local teams."

Elvis stumbled back into his chair. The sky was cloudy and damning. It brightened for a moment as lightning came rippling down in the distance near his tiny pizzeria. "How... what... *What have you done*? You never even took my picture!" Elvis stared at the logo for a while. He briefly contemplated hurling Little Jim over the balcony. Elvis was pretty sure that he could lift the tiny man up and chuck him as easily as a sack of potatoes.

"We pulled some shots off your social media, and my graphics guys did the rest. That's actually Chris Hemsworth's torso. *That* was a pretty penny. But you're worth it, buddy. We're already putting up the new signs on your location. My team is in there right now, changing the layout to make it a little more family friendly." Jim looked at his watch. "Well, you should get going, Elvis. Bunch of hungry people out there will be putting in orders soon. It's an exciting game, but not a terribly long one. We have pizzas to knock out. Oh, not to worry, I don't expect you to handle that volume on your own. Coach Pecante and the team are reporting to you immediately following the game. All the kids know is that they're getting free pizza and pop. My staff at the new kiosk here will take some of the pressure off your location, too." Jim saw some birds in the distance and picked up his gun. "It's going to be a nice evening after all."

Elvis willed himself up from the chair. Then his legs automatically carried him towards the elevator.

Little Jim raised the gun and pulled the trigger. He caught

two birds simultaneously as they criss-crossed in the air. The two birds fell, one of them thudding into the cart of a tall, skinny guy dressed in drag. The other hit one of the spectators sitting in the parking lot. Jim concerned himself for a fraction of a second, but quickly realized that the spectator, who was gesturing wildly and shouting profanity skyward, was totally fine.

Then Jim laughed hysterically.

Elvis envied the birds.

-12-

Automatic Elvis automatically stopped halfway to the elevator and automatically said, "I'm going to need more cheese."

Little Jim laughed. "That's the spirit! Don't worry. It's taken care of. Everything's good to go, you'll see. Have fun tonight. Welcome to the team! You'll see — I take care of my own. Little Jim's got you covered."

Automatic Elvis automatically got in the elevator and automatically pressed the button. The doors closed. When they opened again, he automatically stepped out and looked around the store as the last of the shoppers gathered their belongings from the self-checkout terminals.

A shopper dressed as a pedestal lamp was having difficulties getting the checkout scanner to read the barcode on a frosted-over, sixty-dollar ham. He abandoned the ham on the floor and began frantically scanning assorted candy bars from the impulse rack until he'd filled enough crevices in the cart to meet the weight quota.

Loretta stopped him before he could leave. With crossed arms, she chirped, "Hey! And just who do you think is going to put that ham away? Chop chop. Time's tickin'!"

He rushed the ham to the very back of the store and haphazardly tossed it in the freezer. He could hear the crowd as it began counting down from ten. He ran to his cart and shoved it past Loretta, sneering at her over his shoulder.

Automatic Elvis followed him out, automatically.

The crowd chanted, "Three... two... one... GO!" and the shoppers began running.

Elvis slowly walked behind the dashing lamp. It was so beautiful out. Black clouds permeated the sky. Rain fell onto his golden locks of hair. He calmly walked towards his pizzeria. The lamp ahead of him seemed to be running so slowly. Everything was happening in slow motion. When did lamps start shopping? Everything was changing so quickly. People kept moving his cheese.

Behind Elvis, both teams streamed out of the store in much faster motion.

From a bag boy's perspective, the game was easy. Hit the people who have carts. Don't hit the people who don't have carts. Do what the coach says.

They streamed past Elvis like minnows parting around a stone.

The late-leaving lamp ran as fast as it could, but it wasn't fast enough. Big Jesse considered tackling him but veered off for more promising targets at Coach Pecante's behest, while another Hare was tasked with taking the slowpoke down.

Automatic Elvis watched the lamp smash its face against its cart when a Hare took it down at the knees. Automatic Elvis walked as gunshots echoed behind him and birds dropped from the sky. When did lamps start having faces? Clocks had faces. But not lamps. When did lamps get knees?

The rain started coming down harder, slicking the road.

A chicken pushing a cart full of fresh turkeys skidded into one of the many terrible potholes, securely lodging the cart. An opposing bag boy tackled the bird from the side, spilling chicken and turkey onto the street.

The seagulls came furiously from above, swarming down on the meat, tearing through cellophane to the flesh.

Automatic Elvis looked to the sky. The blimp's screen flipped over to an enormous picture of stupid-looking, half-naked Elvis, in his stupid apron and his stupid hat. The rest of the walk was a blur. Automatic Elvis's thoughts dwelled on cheese, warped shopping carts, and football. When he got to his store, Big Jesse was outside, posing for a drone beside a tipped cart. Elvis looked up at his new canopy and sign. The work crews were just strapping the ladders back onto a big white van. They'd put giant logos on the crystal-clear glass front, too. Elvis walked inside to find that nearly nothing was the same. The decor and menu were different. The tables and chairs had changed. The walls were freshly painted in bright, tacky colours. The only familiar thing left in his pizzeria were the automatic drink dispensers. They'd installed a point-of-sale system, with integrated online ordering. Demands for pizza were coming in faster than Elvis could count them.

A family of four walked in. The little boy, holding his mother's hands, shouted, "Hey look! It's *Energetic Elvis*! Like from the commercial! That's a good costume!"

The point-of-sale system dinged with each new order.

The little boy asked, "So... is our pizza done, dude?"

Everyone in town had watched the game. Everyone in town was ordering pizza. Elvis panicked and hid in the walk-in cooler.

Fifteen minutes later, Coach Pecante showed up with the team. Some of the boys had experience in pizzerias, and Hektor even knew how to use that particular point-of-sale system. Hektor and Jesse tended the front of the store, while Coach Pecante brought the rest of the brigade back to start making pizzas.

About an hour had gone by before the first break between customers, then Hektor got up from his stool and said, "This is bullshit. Bullshit! I should be drunk already, with my face between someone's legs." He pointed to the display screen. "Have you got this shit figured out yet, Jesse? I need to hang a piss."

Big Jesse sat on his stool behind the counter. The front of the store was filled with people noisily eating. Most of the tables were a mess. The point-of-sale system glowed dimly, casting a pale orange light over Jesse's face. "Yeah, I got this." He didn't know what Hektor was so mad about. They were getting overtime and free pizza. Jesse was hoping he could even sneak one home at the end of the night.

Hektor went into the back to do his thing.

Jesse stared into the orange screen. It slowly burned his retinas.

"It'll be okay," Horatio told him.

Big Jesse looked around the storefront full of young people getting their eat-on, putting something into their guts to soak up the liquor from the bars they'd be heading to afterwards.

"I'm behind on my rent," Jesse lamented quietly, well below the threshold required to break through the ambiance of the music and the crowd. "Always behind. I miss the way things were," he muttered into the orangeness.

Horatio considered the old, eroded brick of the brewery across the street. "It's a big world out there. I'm still not sure if anyone is truly happy. Maybe the ones who die with smiles on their faces just managed to fake them their entire lives. What's one more smile at the end?"

Big Jesse sighed.

Hektor returned from the bathroom and plopped his ass back onto his stool. "Did I miss anything?"

Jesse shook his head and kept staring into the orange light.

Hektor hadn't washed his hands after taking his piss, but considering he'd been handling physical currency — the most disgusting thing in the universe — he didn't really care.

During the course of the night, there would be seventy-nine specific usages of the staff bathroom: five phone calls outside of scheduled work breaks, thirteen defecations, forty-six urinations, twelve pot vaporization sessions, two vomiting episodes, and once for the purpose of masturbation.

Some of those usages were combined — for instance, vomiting followed by urination (or both, simultaneously) during the same visit. Of fifty-three unique visits to the facility, hand washing was involved in twenty-six of them. I could bore you by sharing how many of the boys didn't use the bathroom at all, or how many just took a piss on the side of the dumpsters because some asshole was busy jerking off in the only bathroom, but we certainly don't have time for all *that*. I *will* say that the guy who jerked off *did* wash his hands. Kudos to him. Unfortunately, he washed them *before* he did the self-nasty, and not after. I suppose we'll give him half points on that one.

The person who vomited twice was Elvis. He'd leave the safety of the cooler, do his business in the bathroom, and retreat. He curled up in a corner of the cooler and stared up into the steel ceiling with his phone clutched in his hand. He had texts from every contact in his list, and several more from numbers he didn't recognize. He ignored all but one, to which he fired off a quick reply. Help was on the way.

Coach Pecante walked into the freezer. He crossed his arms

and stared down at Elvis. "I still don't know why you're hiding in here. Some people just can't handle the spotlight. My mama always told me, if you can't handle the heat, cook faster. You just gotta cook faster, son! The sooner you're done cookin', the sooner you can turn off the oven."

Elvis didn't even look him in the eye. He just kept staring at the label on a box of cheap cheese sitting beside him. The cheese came from Little Jim's store, as did the pepperoni, the tomatoes, the flour, and every other ingredient. He parted his blue, frosty lips, croaking out, "How's the pizza?"

The coach shrugged. "M'eh. The kids seem to like it." He closed the steel door behind him with a loud thud. The light went off.

Elvis sat in the dark and shivered for a while. Eventually, the door opened and the light came back on, revealing Eric in the doorway.

Eric shook his head disapprovingly. "Having fun down there?"

"Help me up, asshole."

Eric stooped down, lifting Elvis off of the cold steel floor. They hobbled out the back of the store and plopped into the chairs, after kicking two Hares out of them.

Elvis looked half-dead — until he saw his car. His eyes went wide. The new logo was on the side of his beloved El Camino. His jaw clenched and saliva began leaking from the corners of his mouth. One of his eyes started twitching. His rage was remarkably palpable in the silence.

Eric stayed silent, too, but it was more of a *I wonder if I should leave quietly, or if I should call an ambulance and then leave quietly* type of silence.

This went on for a while, until they both asked, "Why am I here, man?" at the exact same moment.

Elvis snapped out of it. He told Eric everything. He started by telling him about the shit-bag lawyer who'd pilfered his cash float and fast-talked his hungover ass into signing his life away. The whole world watched as things went downhill from there. He talked for an hour straight, allowing Eric no opportunity to interrupt.

Eric nodded along until Elvis was finally finished. Then Eric slowly said, "I'm surprised you didn't mention the commercial."

What little blood that had returned to Elvis's face quickly dissipated. "Commercial? Right... the little kid said something about a commercial. I haven't seen it."

Eric loaded up the video on his phone. "They started airing the new version literally the minute the game ended." He hit play and passed it to Elvis. "Sixty-five million views and counting."

The commercial began with fast-forwarded drone footage of the bag boys driving around in the purple El Camino, wearing long blond wigs while they made deliveries. But then it transitioned to drone footage from outside Little Jim's Grocery Store at the beginning of the game:

Queen's "We Will Rock You" plays in the background. The straggling lamp runs frantically, pushing his cart towards the camera. Big Jesse cuts around him, then zips past the drone. The lamp gets taken down brutally from behind. His mouth shatters on the handlebar in spectacular, ultra-high-definition fashion. Elvis walks out the store into the carnage, looking at it indifferently. The camera pans to him, wide at first, tightening to a medium headshot. His hair blows in the wind like a Nordic god, while he passes through pandemonium. A brilliant bolt of lightning touches down in the distance behind him. The new logo fades in, as Elvis slowly walks away from the store.

Elvis slumped into his chair. "I think I've made a mistake."

"Think?" Eric sneered. "Listen, man. I'm sorry, but you're way too public now. I came tonight as a favour, but this is the last time. You're going to have to get the legal shit after this."

Elvis pouted. "But the legal stuff isn't nearly as good as the stuff you get."

Eric shrugged. "Price you pay for fame, brah. I don't even want to be here right now, man. Those fucking drones could be anywhere." Eric looked around cautiously. "We'll text. Good luck. And don't forget the little people."

Elvis looked shocked. "For real? You're just gonna bail and we're not gonna hang anymore?"

"Sorry man. We're all looking out for number one." He smiled sardonically, adding, "Hey. Don't worry. It's been fun, man. Okay? No hard feelings. See you on the screens." He slung his backpack over his shoulder and left.

Elvis opened the lid of the cooler. He knew he'd forgotten to put fresh ice in it, though at that moment he'd have been content with warm beer. When he reached in, there was nothing but empties and a used condom. He went and got the bottle of rye he kept hidden in his office and went back outside to sit. He wished he had a cigarette.

-13-

E lvis woke up hungover again.
　　He tried to let the nausea pass. For one brief moment, in his state of general hungover-ness he couldn't remember ever having met Little Jim. For that moment, he was in a different universe, and his pizzeria was the same as it had been before he met the tiny tyrant. Then it all came flooding back to him. He leaned over and vomited into the cooler. The cooler had seen better days. So had Elvis. He dry-retched until his ribs were sore. Then he slumped back into the chair. For a little while he thought about killing himself, then he pulled out his phone to check the time.

It was 2:09 in the afternoon. He had 1,208 unanswered texts. Everyone wanted answers. He scrolled down the list. His elderly mother, who was living down in Florida, had sent 177 of them. He replied, *I'm fine, talk to you soon.* Then he deleted the entire conversation and resolved to call her when he was in better condition.

Little Jim had sent him one text — it read: *You photograph so well.* Elvis didn't quite know what to make of that. One other text caught his attention above the rest. It was from Melanie, Eric's ex-girlfriend. *What's going on over there? You fall off the map, then this? What the fuck, Elvis?*

Elvis dialed her number.

She answered the line after six long rings. "What do you want?"

"Hi, Mel," he groaned.

"You sound like shit."

Elvis managed a faint laugh. "Yeah, I know. I also look like shit and feel like shit." He hoped to hear a laugh from the other end of the line. He didn't.

"I thought we were friends?"

"We are. I just... I got busy. The pizzeria, then all of this. It was so sudden." Elvis was met with more silence. He added, "Speaking of being friends... What happened with Eric? I thought things were good there. You should have texted me."

"The hell do you care? I hadn't heard from you in months." She started crying. "You used to send me beautiful texts. You always had such a way with words. We'd talk about things. Not like with him. He's so quiet with women. With me. When you were around, though, it was different. He spoke more."

"So, you're mad that I stopped texting you and hanging out with you guys? I don't know what to tell you, Mel. I wasn't talking to Eric at the time, either. You know that. I was so busy. It wouldn't have felt right to be texting you more than him."

"You're such an asshole. He and I had a good thing going. Don't you get it, though? You were a part of that. You bridged the gap for us. You fucked everything up when you bought that fucking shithole. And now all this."

Elvis could hear her crying. "What happened with Eric?"

"You're such a fucking character, Elvis. Just leave me alone."

"Why did you bother texting me if you won't tell me what happened?"

She slowly got control of her crying. "He was fucking me... and I was staying still for him. With my eyes closed. Like always. You know. Doing my thing. But there was just... there was nothing. I didn't feel anything. Usually it felt good, y'know? But this time, it was so cold. And I think he could feel it, too. Because he was taking forever to come. I just… I wanted to feel something. He started fucking me so hard that it started to hurt. It didn't feel right, coming from him." She began sobbing.

"I don't understand."

"See, I tried to relax… to think about something else, just so I could feel something. And for a second… I thought about you."

They were both silent for a moment.

"So," Elvis asked, "That's when you moaned?"

"Yes."

"I didn't know you felt that way."

"Well… neither did I. Goodbye, Elvis." She hung up.

Elvis put his phone down and stared into the distance. He reached under the chair, pulled out the binoculars, and looked towards the tower. He stared at it hatefully while he thought evil thoughts. He put the binoculars away and lurched to his feet. He went to the bathroom to clean himself up. Then he remembered the logo on the side of his beloved El Camino. He went back outside to take a closer look. The logo wasn't actually painted on — it was just a magnetic sticker. It was the first good news he'd had in a while. He peeled it off and was about to toss it in the back seat when he noticed three used condoms on the dashboard. He spun around angrily, hurling the logo like a discus towards the garbage bins. The logo turned broadside and clung perfectly to the side of the steel box. Energetic Elvis stared back at Suicidal Elvis.

Elvis got into the car. It smelt of sweat and sex, but not the familiar smell of his own sweat and sex. He reached into the glove compartment, rooting around until he found a handful of fast-food napkins. He used them to peel the sticky condoms from the dash.

If you'd like to know who the condoms belonged to, the answer is three different bag boys on the team, who'd all taken turns fucking the same young smooth fanboy. None of the guys were Jesse, and none of them were Hektor, though I suppose one of them *could* have been Hektor, because he'd certainly banged that piece of ass in the past. Elvis went out the back gate without bothering to lock it behind him. He marched slowly towards Little Jim's tower. The sun was behind it, casting a long shadow down the street. He'd have made a great Roman soldier. Down the potholed road he trudged towards the capital.

When he arrived, Loretta looked up from her phone briefly to greet him. "He's in the tower," she told him. Behind her, people lined up at the self-checkout terminals.

"Beep, boop, beep," said the checkouts.

Elvis went up the tower and found Jim on the balcony.

Little Jim looked Elvis up and down with a critical eye. "You don't look well," Little Jim said. "Have a seat."

"You turned me into a fucking clown."

"I did no such thing," Jim said. "You're very presentable. Men would kill to have those golden locks. Women would kill to be with the man who has them. Kids look up to you."

"You changed everything."

"I don't know how you were staying afloat, using all those imported ingredients. This is much more cost effective."

Elvis straightened up in his chair and said, "You told me everyone would be eating my pizza! This isn't *my* pizza! This is *your* pizza!"

Little Jim laughed. "We did well last night. All eight locations picked up more than enough sales to offset the freebies we sent out. Have you checked your bank account yet? Your first deposit went in."

Elvis took out his phone and logged in to his bank account. His jaw dropped. "That was from *one* night?"

"This sport is proving to be more and more profitable," Jim mused.

Elvis stared at his phone. "I can spend this?"

"I don't know, can you?"

Elvis looked confused.

Little Jim sighed. "Yes, you can spend it." He stood up. "I was about to head down to see my head cashier. Come, you can ride with me." They both walked to the elevator. Inside, the confined space amplified Elvis's general stench. Jim inhaled in a very deliberate manner. He sniffed again and said, "Is that going to be a problem, Elvis? Our brand needs to be well represented. You're in the limelight now."

Elvis said nothing. He sucked up his pride and nodded.

The elevator stopped and opened.

Little Jim touched Elvis on the arm. "Have a good day, Elvis. Come to the game next week. I'd like a repeat performance of that walk you took when the game began. It was very... dramatic." He beckoned for Loretta, who was happily playing on her phone.

She instantly looked less happy when she saw Jim walking towards her.

Little Jim looked back over his shoulder, telling Elvis, "We'll make a tradition of it maybe, eh?" Jim came alongside Loretta and took her gently by the arm, leading her towards his office.

Elvis started walking back to the pizzeria. He was different, somehow. He just couldn't quite figure out how, or why.

Business on all fronts continued as usual. The playoffs came and went. The Hares finished with a perfect season, earning their second Dented Cart Trophy. Little Jim placed it in the front window of the store, beside the first one.

The off-season was an eventful one.

For Elvis, the winter was a white fog. He watched his bank account fill up while he drank just enough not to be drunk and smoked just enough cannabis to take the edge off his misery. He rarely answered his texts and the only people he still talked to were his mom and Little Jim. Melanie texted him from time to time. If the crippling depression hadn't kept his dick limp, he might have texted her back. He just didn't have the will.

Eric kept being Eric. He hadn't seen Elvis all winter, but he occasionally sent him unanswered texts, like, *Did you know that America consumes two billion dollars' worth of mayonnaise per year and one billion worth of ketchup? Think about it!* That was one of the more light-hearted ones. Most of them had to do with imminent stock market collapse and government corruption. Eric had a political science degree from his younger days, which is a different way of saying that Eric paid a lot of money to make himself insane. Part of the reason Elvis never answered his texts was because they only served to depress him further.

For Jesse, the reduced hours during the off-season really put him behind. His landlord was a pretty decent guy and had let the late rent slide for a while, but eventually, he'd had no choice but to evict. Big Jesse moved back into his parents' basement.

Coach Pecante used the early part of winter to pick up some quick cash doing advertising gigs. The coach was every advertiser's dream — a naive, walking billboard. They compensated him handsomely to hawk antiperspirant, tires, and the like. He spent his time and money in Mexico, where he could afford to do cocaine and keep a harem of colourful trans people. By Charlie Sheen's standards, it's probably fair to say that he had the best off-season out of anyone. He came back looking like Mr. Clean on steroids.

The Thin Woman continued her slow journey to recovery. She ditched the wheelchair, opting to struggle with a walker to get around. Her kids were happy to have her back in their dilapidated house, where they could live their dilapidated lives. She thought about revenge a lot — nothing particularly convoluted. Just stealing a cement truck and driving it through the front of Little Jim's store. She envisioned running over Big Jesse then throwing Little Jim into the spinning barrel and watching him drown in the concrete.

Mrs. Tannenbaum continued being a vegetable, and Little Jim continued dumping his emotional waste into her void, just as she had with her late husband.

Jim kept the rules of the game the same but leveraged his assets everywhere he could, starting with a further expansion of the league. The second season proved profitable enough that he justified adding eight teams for the '24 season. I won't bore you with the names of the teams, because in '25, he'd expand the league to thirty-two teams, and in '26, to sixty-four. Damned if I'm going to list all those teams. If you want a superfluous listing of items, refer to any page of any George R. R. Martin novel that involves a feast.

The extra traffic coming in and out of Little Jim's store had really been a detriment to the already crumbling roads. Hanmer, on the outskirts of the 3,200-square-kilometre clusterfuck amalgamation known as the Greater City of Sudbury, wasn't high up on the priority list for roadwork. When he called city bureaucrats to complain, they told him as much. Jim priced out repaving the roads from the store to the end zones. The cost was staggering, but within his reach. Rather than do the work piecemeal, one lane at a time, one route at a time, Jim brought in all the demo equipment and crews one Friday evening, and they quickly ripped up all the existing pavement and sidewalks before anyone could stop them. Sudbury's city council was furious. They sent some dweeb in a little white truck and a little yellow helmet to scold Little Jim. "You had no permits!" he yelled. "You gave no notice! People live on these roads! How do you expect them to get around?"

"I don't care," Jim said. "They'll manage. In a week, there will be all new roadbeds, all new pavement, and they will have pristine sidewalks as far as the eye can see. Which beats what you morons do! You'd piece this one job out for the next twelve years, fuck up traffic the whole while, and pay fifty times more to do it wrong than I am to do it right!"

"That's not the point! Do you have any idea how many permits you need to do all this? You can't just rip up public property!"

"Why not? I live on this land! You goddamned idiots haven't done anything to fix the roads! Why are you even *here*? You knew what I'd done. So now the city is wasting more money, sending you out here in your stupid little truck to tell me I didn't have a goddamned permit? While gas is a buck sixty a litre? Go back to your goddamned City Hall, in the faraway goddamned land of Sudbury, where you can waste more of my goddamned tax dollars!"

The city employee turned tail, got back into his city truck, and fled south.

A week later, the roads for half a klick in all directions around Little Jim's Grocery Store were the nicest in the city of Greater Sudbury. Even the residents who'd been inconvenienced by the work couldn't help but appreciate the result.

Without the potholed, shitty roads ripping their vehicles apart, shoppers were willing to make their way to Jim's store more often. He began drawing customers away from the good grocery store across town. Jim put other things into motion, too. He forced the other team owners to turn their stores into LJ franchises. Each store duplicated the layout at Jim's location: bleachers, an owner's tower, and a Pizza Pi! kiosk.

Little Jim was never the type to stop looking up.

That said, he hadn't actually accumulated *nearly* enough money to finance everything he'd done. He'd leveraged the earnings and assets he'd acquired, including the league itself, against massive, long-term, low-interest loans. He'd always bring Elvis to the meetings with the financiers. Who could deny the golden locks and big blue eyes of Energetic Elvis?

Not content to be at the same level as the other team owners, he designed a fifty-foot addition to his own tower, topped with a large private suite: "The Commissioner's Spire." The original LJ's was shut down for a month prior to the new season to accommodate the massive renovation. Jim stayed on the premises the entire time, overseeing the top-secret construction zone. The slick spire sprouted solidly from the existing tower: a smooth, skyward erection. The new penthouse suite didn't jut out from one side of the tower as Jim's old one below did. The new suite was round: fifteen metres in diameter, with a domed roof. It had a small balcony, inset on the side facing the parking lot. After the renovation was complete, some people said the new tower looked like a giant penis with a mushroom head. Others called it a buttplug on a stick.

Jim christened The Commissioner's Spire before the opening

game of the third season. They shattered a bottle of cheap champagne from the store's wine nook against the railing of the balcony. Damned if he'd waste good bubbly. The inside of the new suite was truly luxurious. The high ceiling made the space seem far grander than it actually was. When Elvis first stepped off the elevator, his eyes were immediately drawn to the black marble bar top. It glistened like ice and was nearly as shiny as the young, handsome bartender standing behind it. The mahogany shelves behind *him* were full of top-quality liquor from the bottom shelf up.

The space was both bright and reserved; classic, yet promising to look beautiful for eternity. There were six barstools, big-screen televisions everywhere, and two immaculate, brand new pool tables, balls ready to be broken, and two spindle racks of cues. Automatic sliding glass doors opened onto the inset balcony, where there were only three connected seats. The one in the centre was higher, larger, and far more elaborate than the two flanking it.

Elvis walked over to the antique pool cue racks. Neither of the brass racks was quite the same, but they were both of similar style: they stood upright, spun around, and held ten cues each, a mix of old and new sticks. Some were worn down from years of play. Others had yet to be stroked. One cue in particular caught his eye: a two-piece with a shiny chrome joint, brilliant blue winding, and white marble inlay. The very bottom of the butt was black marble, with a small logo of a faded white falcon in a triangle. He picked it up with great interest and held it in his hands. "Where did you get these cues?"

Jim sidled over to the bar. "Bruce, get me a martini, will you? And I'm sure you recognize our guest? Make sure you attend to his every need as you would my own."

Bruce reached for the vodka. "Absolutely, Jim. Anything I can get you, Elvis?"

Elvis was still holding the cue. He looked at it; weighed it in his hands. Then he laid it on the table, rolling it back and forth on the cloth. He peered down at the cue, scrutinizing it. He turned it over, looking at the other side.

Jim took a seat at the bar. "Something wrong with the cue, Elvis?"

"You didn't answer my question."

"Hmm? Oh. I have no idea. Bruce, you were here when the guy came to install the tables, right?"

"Yes, sir," Bruce said. "He brought some new cues and some old ones, but he said there wasn't a single one in the mix worth less than half a grand. Oh — except the ones tucked under the tables with the rakes. He said those are just heavy sticks for breaking, if you don't want to warp the expensive ones."

Elvis bent over, lifting the break cue from the side of the table. He chalked up carefully, considerately, covering the tip in a thick grit. He walked to the table beside him, leaving the blue cue on the first table. He repositioned the cue-ball to his liking. He took a break stance, flattening his body, stretching out like a cat ready to pounce. Then he leapt forward, crushing the cue-ball. The rack exploded. Sixteen balls cascaded around, until the seven-ball dropped in the corner. Then the thirteen trickled in the side pocket. As the balls slowed, the six-ball rolled slowly towards the corner closest to Elvis. It stopped right at the edge of the pocket, stubbornly refusing to go in.

Bruce slid a martini over to Jim, and enthusiastically exclaimed, "Nice break, sir!"

Jim slowly clapped his hands and raised an eyebrow. "Not your first break, I see. I wish I could break with that much force."

Elvis nodded understandingly. "I used to play a lot." He returned the break cue to its spot then retrieved the blue cue. He stalked around the table, charting a course while he chalked up. The cue-ball had locked against the nine-ball near the centre of the table, cutting off most of his shots. The only sure-make was the six, hanging precariously over the corner pocket.

Jim looked over Elvis's options. "Pretty bleak. Nice break, ugly result. Not much to shoot. Only easy shot is the six, but if you take solids, then you've got that cluster of the two, three, and five to navigate through, downtable. If you're playing one side of an eight-ball game, that is. If you're just shooting stick, have at 'er."

"Mmm-hmm. I think I can make a run out on solids here." Elvis leaned over the table, preparing to make a shot. He took a deep breath, closed his eyes, and made his backstroke, sliding the cue through his bridged fingers. He opened his eyes and smiled, striking the cue-ball solidly. It hustled across the felt to the corner, popped the six in, then back-spun hard towards the cluster of solids, smacking them and breaking them apart. He proceeded to pick off the solids one by one. He pocketed the eight, then dropped the remaining stripes for good measure. He didn't miss once. He walked over to Jim and handed him the cue. "Run your hand up the shaft."

Jim did as asked. One spot caught his attention. He rubbed it back and forth through his fingers. "That's odd. It's like someone took a pin and dug a tiny hole in the side. You can feel it, right there." He frowned. "That's kind of annoying. I wouldn't want to play with it. Maybe we should get the billiards guy to give us a replacement."

Elvis laughed. "That's not what happened to it, though. At

least, it wasn't a pin." Elvis sat on a barstool and took the cue back from Jim. "One time at a pool hall, I leaned this cue against the wall. A drunk guy walked by and accidentally kicked it over. I didn't think much of it. When I took my next shot, it felt like something stabbed my finger. There was a sharp pebble lodged in the wood. I had to pick it out with my fingernail. It left a distinct impression." He firmly took the cue in both hands, giving it a hard twist, popping the joint. It was stiff, not having been broken for a while. He unscrewed the two halves. "I still have the carrying case this came in, you know. Transmission blew on the El Camino. Had to pawn this Falcon to get it on the road again. Shit. That must have been twenty years ago. I eventually got the money together and went back to the pawn shop, but I was too late. They'd already sold it."

Bruce beamed. "Wow! Imagine coming across it all these years later! That's some mighty fine luck! I think that's deserving of a drink! How about a martini?"

Elvis sat there, holding his shaft in one hand and his butt in the other. Although, technically, he was holding Jim's shaft, and Jim's butt, and they both knew it. "Well, Jim?"

"Well, what?" Jim answered. "You haven't asked me anything yet."

"You're really going to make me stand here with my dick in my hand after I said all that? Do I really have to ask, Jim? I've jumped through some pretty big hoops these past months. Give me this one. Please."

Jim smiled. "The colour of the butt matches your eyes."

The room suddenly became very tense, as neither said anything.

Bruce, obliviously young and pretty, asked, "So, what'll it be, then, Elvis?"

Elvis ceased the staring match with Jim, asking, "Bruce, is it?"

"Yessir. I can make a mean margarita, if you'd like. If you want something stiff, we have everything you can imagine. Just name it."

Jim gave Elvis a sinister smile. "Bruce here graduated top of his mixology class. What was it, Bruce? A class of sixty?"

"Yessir, valedictorian. And I've worked all the hot spots in Montréal. I can make you anything you'd like, Elvis, sir. Anything at all."

Elvis looked at Jim. Jim looked at Elvis.

"Bruce," Elvis said, "Listen carefully. I want a double-vodka screwdriver in a tall glass. A chilled glass is preferable, if you have one, as is chilled vodka. Pour in the vodka, then add juice until the glass is half full. Throw in three maraschino cherries and stir. Then add crushed ice. Crushed, but not pulverized, understand? And it'd better damn well be pulp free, good-quality orange juice, and even better-quality vodka."

Bruce winked at Elvis. "Absolutely! A man who knows what he wants! Coming right up!" He clapped his hands and set to work.

Elvis forced another smile at Jim. "Well, Jim? How about it?"

"How about what, Elvis?"

"The cue," Elvis sneered.

"What about it?" Jim crossed his arms and gave Elvis a toothy, wide smile.

Elvis took a deep breath and kept forcing that smile that he'd been forcing for many months. He put the cue back together, and through barely parted lips, asked, "May I have the cue, Jim?"

"I'll tell you what, Elvis," Jim mused, "we'll keep it here it on the property. You can come use it whenever you like. I'll even tell other people not to touch it. If we ever part ways, you can take it with you. Sound good?"

Elvis wanted to be stunned. He wanted to. But he couldn't. He couldn't because he'd come to know what a little prick Jim could be. He took his spoonful of shit. "Fine, Jim," he said, forcing another smile while he gripped the cue so tightly that any sudden movement would surely snap it in half. "Have it your way. I have your word on that?"

"Of course, Elvis. My word is always gold. Haven't I proven that already?"

Elvis continued to hold his forced smile. "You sure have, Jim. You sure have."

Bruce finished making Elvis's drink, sliding it neatly to the edge of the bar.

Elvis set the cue roughly on the bar, picked up his glass and took a sip. He nodded approvingly. "That's not bad, Brucey-boy."

"Thanks, Elvis, sir."

"Bruce," Elvis said, "just call me Sir. I like it better when you just call me Sir."

Jim led Elvis out to the spire's balcony. When the glass doors parted, a strong gust of air blew in. It was much windier than the pre-existing balcony below. Elvis walked up to the railing and leaned gingerly against it, peering over the edge. "Long way down."

Little Jim nodded. "Think you'd die if you jumped?"

Elvis sneered. "It's what, a hundred metres to the ground? Of course you'd die."

"Actually, this level is a hundred and fifty. The lower box is a hundred dead even, from the pavement."

"That's precise."

"I know," Jim said. "That's how I like things."

"Precise?"

"Mmm-hmm." Jim stood on his tippy-toes at the balcony but could just barely see over the side. "Be a sport, Elvy, boy. Lift me up a little so I can get a clear view down." Elvis did as he was asked, hugging Little Jim around the waist and hoisting him up about a foot. Little Jim took his time taking in the landscape while Elvis laboured. "Hey," Little Jim said, "I can see your shop from here." Elvis put Little Jim back down. Little Jim brushed himself off and sat in his new, customized chair. It had digital panels built into each armrest, along with several buttons and controls.

Elvis took his place at Little Jim's side. He thought about all the money being continuously deposited into his account from his share of all the Pizza Pi! outlets. He thought about getting a private little island, or just a strip of beach somewhere in the Caribbean. But he had commitments to Little Jim, and Pizza Pi!, and the Hares. Appearances had to be made. Hands shook. Smiles forced. He'd spent the off-season developing a truly wonderful cannabutter-infused dough recipe. It got him through the days.

Jim asked, "So, you like my little man-cave?"

"Huh?" Elvis asked. "Man-cave? Sure. It's an eagle's nest. But these seats are too low to the railing. We can't even see the game unless we're standing up."

Jim looked genuinely perplexed. "Who the hell cares about the game?" He shook his head in disbelief. "Game," he muttered, picking up his gun from beside the chair.

Elvis didn't know what to say. He just wanted Jim to stop talking so he could go back to his perpetual waking dream where he was anyone but himself. "It's great, then, Jim. What more can I say?"

"You haven't seen anything yet." He pushed a button on the control panel, and the middle panel of the railing in front of them unlocked. The panel slid back and to the side, resting behind the panel next to it. A six-foot-wide catwalk appeared from beneath the deck, slowly extending out into the open air, reaching several metres past the balcony of the suite below.

"What the hell is that for?"

"You'll see. A few legal technicalities to work out yet." He pushed the button again, and the long catwalk withdrew beneath the deck. The railing panel slid back over and locked into place.

Elvis pondered the catwalk. He pondered his life. "The birds don't come up this high as often."

"Yeah, I know. Luckily, there's a solution for everything." He pushed another button on the control panel.

"What's that one do?"

Jim smiled.

Elvis caught a whiff. "Christ, what is that?"

"There's a compartment full of rotten meat above us. I just opened it."

It didn't take long for the seagulls to swarm the spire, swirling around it in a cyclone of flying filth. Jim began firing at will.

Elvis asked, "What are you doing with the old balcony?"

"Leasing it. Goes on the market tomorrow. I'm told there are a lot of wealthy Cart Massacre fans willing to pay top dollar for that suite."

Elvis nodded. He went to the side of the railing and peered down at Big Jesse collecting carts in the parking lot. The boy kept looking upwards, trying to avoid being hit by the raining gulls. He pushed the string of carts back towards the store until he vanished from sight.

"Lots of changes coming for this season," Jim said. "Can't sit on our laurels. Have to keep pushing the action."

-14-

The Hares opened their third season with a month-long, four-game road trip across America, with the first game scheduled in Southern California. Coach Pecante loaded his bag boys onto the bus. They picked a trail due west, only crossing into the United States once they hit British Columbia, adding twenty-two hours of driving to the trip, because as the fiercely patriotic coach said, "Damned if I'll drive a minute more in the States than I absolutely have to."

He tuned the FM radio to classic rock whenever he could. He'd whistle along, always slightly out of key. Even noise-cancelling headphones couldn't block his wretched warbling. He'd lecture to the bag boys on game strategy and offensive spirit, and about going at it until the last egg was recovered. "If you have to lick the yolk off the pavement, you lick that yolk."

Big Jesse spent most of his time on the bus listening to trance music.

Horatio worried for Jesse. He'd watch the boy, helplessly. He said, "If only Little Jim would listen to you. You could make things better for everyone. You don't have to just take what life gives you. It's okay to want more."

Jesse frowned and stared out the window.

As the rickety yellow bus sped westward, the team slowly went insane, staring into screens, blowing through data caps and running up overage charges. The bus had a tiny fan blowing on the driver's seat, which didn't really help cool down

Coach Pecante, but didn't keep the team from thinking that it did.

Perception is everything.

When they reached British Columbia, they turned south and kept going. In Southern California, the bus came to a halt on the crowded freeways. Knowing the coach couldn't force the team to push the bus while they were stuck in traffic, one of the bag boys finally piped up regarding their working conditions.

Hektor shouted, "Hey, Coach. How about turning that fan this way? C'mon, man. We're dying back here."

Coach Pecante eyeballed the boy in the rear-view mirror. "Stuff it, Hektor. Don't make me come back there."

Other drivers were out of their vehicles, stretching their legs, since traffic hadn't moved in forty-five minutes.

Hektor stood up. "Hey, c'mon, Coach. Can I at least get off and get some air? C'mon man."

The coach squinted. "Stick your head out the window. Last warning. Sit your ass down. I mean it. I will make your life a living hell, boy. Don't test me."

Hektor pressed his luck. He laughed. "Oh yeah? C'mon, baldie. I'd love to see that. Whatcha gonna do? Blind me with the glare off your shiny head?"

Coach Pecante smirked and coldly focused on Hektor in the mirror.

The rest of the team watched the showdown.

Coach Pecante said, "Step outside with me, Hektor." He reached over and swung the lever, opening the door.

Hektor played along, though at this point his confidence had subsided to an overblown bravado. He followed the coach off the bus. Outside, Hektor foisted his dukes for furious fisticuffs.

Other commuters turned to look.

The coach sneered. "Put your hands down, you idiot." He moved towards Hektor slowly, leaning in to say something privately to him.

Hektor's expression went flatter than the shocks on the old bus. It looked as though someone had kicked him in the sack. "You wouldn't," he whispered. "You *can't*. I had to transfer after that. None of these guys know."

The coach stood back, crossing his arms in front of him. "Why *wouldn't* I? Why *can't* I?"

Hektor considered his options, envisioning two possible futures.

"Well, boy?"

"You're a real bastard."

"Get back on the bus, boy."

Hektor did as he was told.

Coach Pecante followed closely behind.

When Hektor sat down, the bag boy nearest him asked, "What the hell was that all about?"

Instead of answering, Hektor gave the guy a hard, open-palmed slap across the face. Then he yelled, "Shut up! No one talks!"

Horatio laughed in the silence. Nothing ever changed.

Although Hektor would prefer if his secret were kept sacrosanct between him and his coach, for the sake of maintaining *your* grasp on things I'll be a pal and let you in it on what the Coach whispered: The coach told Hektor, "You know what kid? Teachers talk. I remember when you enrolled in my school halfway through the year. See, Mr. Garthy, your old gym teacher, who happens to be a friend of mine y'know, well he called to tell me about the new kid we were inheriting from his school. Something about shitting your pants during a basketball game? He told me it looked like a big ol' greasy taco dinner leaking all the way down to your sweatsocks. Fuck, did I ever laugh. I bet the rest of the guys would love to hear that story. You probably tell it better than I do. What did they call you after? Hektor McShitsHimself? You get your ass back on that bus, boy. I don't want to hear a peep. Not a peep, you hear me? Not from you or any of those other clowns. I'm holding you in charge of that. You keep those fucking dunces in line."

So, the big yellow bus drove on, and on, and on. The games went by in blurs. Big Jesse remembered tackling a shopper in a pink flamingo costume. He brought down an angel with a tiny devil doll on its shoulder. He tackled a hamburger, and a hotdog, and at least three bottles of ketchup. Jesse was very good at his minimum-wage job.

Bag boys could always tell who the local contestants were: the ones who weren't looking for fame, and certainly weren't looking for fortune. They saw *The Cart Massacres* as an opportunity to stretch a paycheque, doubling down on the hope of making it through another week. It was a hard gamble to resist. In the last match of the road trip, against one of the new expansion teams, the Hares were up by $13,213.76 late in the game. Victory was all but assured.

A short, stout, brute of an old woman dressed as a pumpkin hustled with her cart, but her legs could only carry her so fast. As a low-priority target, the coaches of both teams had worked around her, bringing down faster and more valuable carts first. She'd been counting on that. Big Jesse had just taken down a guy in a panda suit near the end zone when he received new orders to intercept her. He jumped back to his feet, leaving the panda limp on the ground. Turning to the target, he reared up to charge.

Horatio said, "You don't have to always blindly follow orders, Jesse."

Jesse hesitated for a second. He took off at a sprint towards the woman, who was forty metres down the road. Horatio had more to say, but Jesse, sprinting onward, didn't hear him. The wrinkled old pumpkin was twenty metres away. A bag boy from the other team charged toward the pumpkin from the opposite direction, fifty metres distant. Jesse didn't see the stout little pumpkin. He only saw the Thin Woman, mocking him. Hurting him. Stealing from his uncle. Horatio screamed at Jesse, begging him to stop. Jesse looked the woman in the eyes, and suddenly he came to a screeching halt at the 460 marker, a split second before he reached her. The cart thumped against him and stopped, abruptly sending the old woman to her ass.

"Oof," the pumpkin said.

The other bag boy was coming in fast, looking for the takedown. He wasn't quite sure why Jesse was standing there idly, but stats were stats, and he wanted to pad his teedee-peegee. Jesse glanced in the cart. It contained a loaf of Italian bread, eggs, milk, jam, honey, asparagus, carrots, a squash, green beans, red bell peppers, a bulb of garlic, an onion, butter, a brick of cheese, and two small T-bone steaks. Atop it all sat a round cake encased in a clear plastic container. Three sacks of potatoes sat beneath it all to satisfy the minimum weight requirement. The cake was fresh from the bakery department, with chocolate icing, yellow trim, and an intricate, hand-gelled picture of a golf cart with an old man driving down the fairway, smiling ear to ear. The writing on the cake read:

Forced Lay-Off / Early Retirement

M'eh.

What's the difference?
We'll make it.
We always have.

Jesse looked down at the woman sitting on her butt. She looked nothing like the Thin Woman. He yelled, "Get off your fucking ass and run!" With the action finished at all the other end zones, the air around them was thick with drones.

Coach Pecante shouted, "What the hell is this? Jesse! What the fuck are you doing?"

Jesse ripped his helmet off and threw it at the opposing bag boy, providing an extra moment of distraction. The woman started to her feet. She was just too goddamned slow. Jesse ran around the cart and practically hoisted her up. The other bag boy was practically on top of them. Beyond that one, other bag boys from both teams were closing in fast. Jesse took a split second to assess the field. Two opposing teams, and one clear directive. Get the ball to the end zone. For once, everything made sense again. He didn't see colours. It was just him, them, and a big orange ball.

The first bag boy tried to deke around him and take the pumpkin from the side. Jesse wasn't fooled, and intercepted him. They crashed together, stumbling towards the old lady, who'd just gotten going again. Jesse clutched the other bag boy, forcing him down. As they skidded across the ground, the opposing bag boy reached out, smacking the cart with enough force to break the old woman's grip and start the cart tipping.

The contents in the cart shifted to the side, bringing it down even faster. It was precariously close to the point of no return when Jesse leapt from all fours, using the other bag boy's face as a springboard, extending his body as much as he possibly could, snatching the cart's rear wheel between the tips of his finger and thumb. He got enough of it to tip it back down onto all four wheels.

Jesse jumped to his feet and pushed the cart to a running start — just fast enough that the woman could keep pace with it. "Run, damn you! RUN!"

He turned around and started slowly walking backwards.

Time slowed down. All he could hear were his own deep breaths. He saw them all coming. Thirty-one metres from the end zone, the next bag boys moved in. The first tried a double-step juke to get around Jesse, who dropped to a low squat, grabbed him 'round the waist, and lifted him high in the air.

"ON YOUR TEN!" Horatio yelled.

Jesse spun around twice and tossed his captive like a discus into the next bag boy. Both bag boys crumpled to the pavement. He quickly dispatched six more bag boys, one after another. Some of Jesse's hits were pretty questionable. Not just by football standards, but by rugby standards, and even alley-brawl standards. Two blood lusting bag boys, one from each team, rushed him as a united front. Jesse bit his lip and charged forward. He leapt into the air, throwing his body sideways into both of them at once. They all came crashing down together. Hektor came rushing in and didn't slow down — he sprung over Jesse and the other two bag boys like a triplet of hurdles. Jesse reached up, grasping for Hektor's leg. He only managed to graze a shoe, but it was enough to foul Hektor's landing.

Hektor stumbled, his hands touched the ground, but he bounded back up and kept going. Jesse rolled out of the mass, coming up to his knees. The crowd around the finish line was silent. No one was sure whether or not they should be cheering. The pumpkin ran, her short little legs pumping as fast as they could. The end zone was just ahead. Hektor chased her, diving at the last possible moment. He got a fistful of orange fabric and grabbed hard. She came down on her ass, again.

The cart rolled into the end zone.

The crowd went wild.

Hektor let her go and walked back towards the store. As he passed Jesse, he said, "I ought to punch you in the fucking face. But coach is in my ear, telling me not to." Instead, Hektor spat on the ground at Jesse's feet. The drones caught it all in stunning definition.

Jesse walked to the end zone. The crowd had already surrounded the pumpkin, helping her to her feet and across the finish line. When the woman noticed him, she very tentatively said, "I don't understand."

Jesse didn't answer. He walked to her cart and looked inside. The cake had tipped over, icing smeared every which way against the inside of the plastic cover. The writing was all but gone. Jesse picked it up and stared at it. "I'm sorry," he said, handing it to her. "Your cake is ruined."

He sat on the ground and cried, surrounded by carts, shoppers, spectators, a pumpkin, twenty-eight drones live-casting to the world, and Horatio.

-15-

The team made it home to Hanmer in great time. They'd have made even better time had Coach Pecante not been pulled over and ticketed for speeding in seven different states. Hektor paced up and down the bus aisle the entire trip, eyeing everyone, daring them to speak. It was a quiet, if tense, ride.

As soon as they arrived at the store in Hanmer, Little Jim escorted Jesse up The Commissioner's Spire and out onto the balcony. Jim sat down, and Jesse took the seat on his left.

Jim picked up his gun, out of habit. "Well, Jesse? Care to explain yourself?"

Horatio said, "You should tell him to go to hell."

Jesse said nothing.

Jim crossed his arms. "Damnit, Jesse. After everything I've done for you. Kept you out of trouble. Hell, I've even spun your atrocities into something positive. But do you have any idea how much money you just cost me? What the hell were you thinking? You've made us look like idiots out there. You really hurt some of those guys. Guys on your own team, too. The fans want answers. Pecante wants answers. *I* want answers."

Jesse looked at the sky, then back at his uncle. "She shouldn't have even been there. She didn't stand a chance. The league doc shouldn't have let her play. Sometimes someone's gotta look out for people like that. It didn't even matter. We'd already won. She was shorter than *you*, for fuck's sake."

Jim bit his lip. "We got disqualified, Jesse! You cost us the game! You cost us the winning streak! We were undefeated through three seasons! What about the rest of the Hares, Jesse? What about them? What about Coach Pecante? What about the fans?"

"I didn't think..."

Jim cut him off. "That's right. You didn't *think*. The other owners are furious. Some of them want you banned for life. Luckily, I was able to talk them down. You're too big an asset to the brand, Jesse. If this was anyone but you, it'd be over. Do you understand? You're suspended for the rest of the regular season. You can put your uniform back on if we make the playoffs."

Jesse didn't say anything.

Little Jim stood up. "I'm really disappointed in you. I have better things to do than be your babysitter. When the Hares take to the parking lot tomorrow, you're sidelined. Got it?"

Horatio observed.

Jesse said nothing.

Coach Pecante addressed the media. He was exhausted, and not entirely on point. "Now," the coach said into the array of microphones, "I won't have a lick of any of you jumping to hasty conclusions, understand me? The speaker's always the loudest right before it blows, know what I'm saying? You," he said, pointing to the closest reporter.

"Coach," the burly man said, "Do you have any explanation for what happened out there? Three of those guys were from his own team, and one of them is out for the season with cracked ribs. The players from the other team got it even worse. Two of those guys' careers are finished."

The coach stroked his chin between his thumb and index finger for a few moments before answering. "You know, sometimes a grenade is full of potential energy, eh? But sometimes, a grenade is thrown a little to the left, or to the right, right? Well, I bet'cha you didn't know this — grenades are the same weight as a baseball because they wanted American soldiers to be familiar with the weight and feel of 'em. And Big Jesse, well, he grew up on football, and didn't bleed blue like some Canucks. So, he really didn't stand a chance out there." Pecante's forehead glistened under the lights. He awkwardly smeared the sweat with his greasy forearm.

The reporter wasn't sure what to say. The whole room was pretty quiet.

"Next question," Pecante barked, pointing to the first reporter who dared put his hand up in the air.

"What does Jim McGee plan to do? We can't just have these boys teeing off on one another like barbarians. Is he going to set an example?"

The coach answered that one from a piece of paper with a few pre-scripted lines. "Commissioner McGee has suspended Big Jesse for the remainder of the regular season." He ended the conference and walked out of the room.

The remainder of the season went by in a flash. Coach Pecante brought on two new high-school footballers from the region and found that neither of them were capable of filling the shoes of Big Jesse. The Hares' first loss quickly turned to two, then three, then four. Little Jim, who cared little enough for the game when his team was winning, suddenly cared a whole lot. After the team returned from a dismal road trip, Jim summoned the coach to his penthouse suite. Coach Pecante had seen the new suite before, when Jim insisted he bask in it. Then Jim hosed him at a game of pool or seven. This time, Little Jim wasn't in such a good mood. He was sitting at the bar, having a martini. Bruce was standing at his post, uncomfortably cleaning the same glass for the thousandth time. He missed the boisterous life he'd left behind in Montréal.

Jim motioned to the seat beside him. "Sit."

The coach walked over and took his place. He thought about ordering a drink, then thought better of it.

"Well," Jim said. "How do you explain this? The first loss is on Jesse. What about the rest?"

Pecante stiffened his spine. "How is this *my* fault? Big Jesse wasn't just *our* best player, he was the top player in the league. And he knocked our third best player out for the season. Americans take sports seriously, Jim. The teams down there have big high-school football programs. They're drawing from a much better pool of players. We're getting killed. Haven't you been following the results? The Canadian teams are *all* getting ransacked by those southern teams."

"Huh," Jim said. He hadn't thought about that. It made sense. He just wasn't sure what to do about it. He was a little sore with himself for not having realized it in the first place. Perhaps the coach wasn't entirely to blame. "Come. Let's shoot a couple games while I ruminate."

Little Jim picked a cue at random from one of the racks. The coach picked Elvis's cue. Little Jim didn't stop him. They played a few games. The coach lost them all compliantly, not that he had any choice in the matter.

They were both standing there, cues in hand, when Jim said, "Here's what we're going to do. I'm going to invest a significant amount of money into high-school sports programs in each

Canadian town with an LJ's and a team. I'll even pump money into the grade schools. Let's also pump some money into their nutritional programs. We'll have better bag boys coming out of the schools in no time."

Coach Pecante said, "But it'll take years before those kids come up through a new program. What do we do until then?"

"Lose gracefully," he replied. "You already know a thing or two about that. It'll all balance out eventually. I've got bigger fish to fry, Coach. Good luck with the team. Sorry to ream you out the way I did."

Suddenly, the elevator opened, and Elvis stepped out of it. "Jim," he started to say, when the cue in the Coach's hands caught his eye. Elvis looked at Jim. "So, I see it didn't take long for you to break your promise."

Jim shrugged. "Slipped my mind, Elvis. There's a lot on it besides sticks. I knew your cue would be in safe hands."

Elvis nodded, smiling like a man who knew he had the upper hand. He walked over to the coach and took the cue from him. "So, it slipped your mind, or you knew it would be in safe hands? Which is it, Jimmy-boy?"

Little Jim was left momentarily speechless, and perhaps even a trifle ashamed of himself — or at the very least, ashamed that he'd been caught breaking one of his own bullshit promises, on account of his utter indifference to Elvis's bullshit desires.

Elvis asked the coach, "Did Jim tell you the story of this cue?" He turned to Jim. "Do you even remember it?"

"Sure," Jim said. "You pawned it years ago to fix your shit-box El Camino. And then you forgot about it. And then I bought it. And now it's mine."

Elvis held the cue in his hands. "That's not quite how I told it." He slid it up and down in his grip. "I never forgot it. Never." He stood silently, enjoying the tension. "I have something to show you. The person who leased the other suite is finished with the renovations. Come see." He turned to the elevator, bringing the cue with him.

Jim gestured to the cue. "Aren't you forgetting to return something?"

Elvis smiled, walked into the elevator, then held the door open with the butt of the cue. "I think you'll like it down there."

Jim and the coach followed him into the elevator. Elvis hit the button for the lower box, and the doors closed. The ride was spent in silence. The doors opened onto an eye-bendingly familiar sight. Elvis stepped into the room. It was a tiny, private paradise. A short black marble bar ran along the left side. The mahogany shelves were full of top-quality liquor from the bottom shelf up. It was both bright and reserved; classic, yet promising to look beautiful for eternity. There were three barstools, a big-screen television, and a single, immaculate, brand new pool table, balls ready to be broken. Beyond that, there was a glass barrier with an automatic door leading onto the balcony, where Elvis had tucked his multi-coloured chairs and cooler from the back of the pizzeria. An antique brass cue rack off to the side of the pool table had a single empty slot. Elvis walked over and slid his cue into it. Then he turned around and gave Jim a smug look. "On the property."

Jim was furious. He could feel his face reddening, though he did his best not to acknowledge that fact. Instead, he smiled and said, "Imitation is the highest form of flattery." He looked around. It was less than half the size of the suite atop The Commissioner's Spire.

The coach laughed. "It's you-sized, Jim."

Jim looked up at the coach. His face got redder. "What the

fuck did you just say?"

"I, uh..." the coach stammered.

Elvis laughed uncontrollably.

Jim considered firing Coach Pecante. He quickly ran the numbers in his head, realizing he'd never find another person to drive a bunch of losers around the continent and babysit them in return for a weekly food voucher. "Get out," he said. "You have work to do. You're playing three Canadian teams on this home stand. Surely you have no excuses for losing those games?"

Coach Pecante nodded. "Yes, sir. No, sir." He bolted for the stairs, thudding downward, disappearing from sight.

Elvis took a seat at his bar. "Well, I wish there was more I could show you. The bathroom's not as big, either. One urinal instead of two. Two stalls instead of four."

Jim didn't budge from the entrance. "What the hell is this, Elvis?"

"Just a *little* place to call my own."

"So, this is what you decided to spend all your money on? For what? There was a place for you fifty metres above us."

"Maybe I like it better down here. The air's not quite as thin."

Jim pointed at the big, blond man. "You'd better be on point for this upcoming home game. We're projecting you holographically to all the stores. You'll be leading the charge for every team in the league. We've got market shares to take a bite from. Pizza Pi! is poised for a huge uptick. Then, maybe we even do an IPO. Worldwide expansion. By the time you cash out your share, you'll be able to buy a small moon orbiting Jupiter."

Elvis nodded. "I'll do my job."

Jim turned to go back to the elevator.

"Oh, Jim," Elvis said. "Make sure you send Bruce down. He

works for me now."

Little Jim turned on his heels. "What are you talking about?"

"I asked him what you were paying him, and I offered to double it."

"And what if I offer him triple?"

Elvis shrugged. "If he's worth that to you, go ahead. To me, he's worth double what you were paying him. Probably not four times, though. Catch you on the flip side, pal." Elvis winked, pointed an imaginary gun at Jim, and pulled the trigger.

Jim got into the elevator and went back up the spire, stewing the entire ride. He clenched his fists and remembered a distant locker room. He closed his eyes, took three deep breaths, forced himself to unclench his fists, and when the doors opened, he looked straight at Bruce. Calmly and quietly, Jim said, "I like you, Bruce. But no bartender is worth what I'd have to pay to keep you."

"I know, sir. I'm sorry. I couldn't *not* take it. I'm sorry. And it just didn't feel right to ask you for more money after he made the offer, either. I'm truly sorry. But I have to think about my future. I can really use that money."

Jim took a deep breath. "I know."

They both stood in silence for a moment.

Bruce spoke first. "I really am sorry, sir. I feel really shitty about all this."

Little Jim looked at the ground and shook his head. "No. You shouldn't. You should take every last penny you get and make a life for yourself. If one moron is willing to give you more of them than the last, you take them and you never look back."

Bruce nodded. "Thank you, sir. I'm glad you're not angry."

Three minutes later, the elevator returned to Elvis's suite, the doors opened, and Bruce walked out. He took his place behind the bar, where he made his new boss a screwdriver without being asked.

Down below them, Loretta was sitting on a stool between self-checkouts seven and eight, so she could get a good view of all the registers at once while she played on her phone. Forty-six people stood in a long queue, waiting for their turn. Two of the checkouts were out of order. The twelfth customer in line thought to herself, *If they had even just one normal checkout, that old hag could get off her ass and check some of us through.* Then she eyed a tabloid magazine on the impulse rack. It had a tight face shot of George Clooney smiling toothily, and a caption that read, "The Next President?" She looked at the abundance of food in her cart. None of it appealed to her at the moment. *I think I'm going to pick up McDonald's on the way home.*

The coach was just exiting the stairwell from his long walk down. He headed for Loretta, forcing his way through several people's carts to get there. All of the male customers and a few of the female customers attempted to give him high fives. Pecante left them all hanging. He went up to Loretta, got close enough to make her uncomfortable, tilted his shiny head down, and asked, "Well?"

She looked up from her phone and glanced around the store. Everything looked normal. "Well, what?"

"Did you know?"

"You're going to have to be more specific than that," she said. Because truth be told, Loretta knew a lot of things. For instance, she knew that if she held up the line for five minutes to reboot the self-checkout system, it would probably bring those two terminals back online. She also knew that she didn't want to hear people gripe for five minutes.

Coach Pecante said, "Don't play stupid with me. How did Elvis snatch up the lease on the old box without Little Jim finding out?"

Loretta's eyes went wide and she instantly put her phone in her pocket. "You have my complete attention."

"*You* didn't know? How could you not have known?"

She shrugged. "Jim told me that it was bought by a numbered company. Then contractors started showing up to renovate it. Why would *Elvis* lease it?"

"I don't know. Something about a stick. Pool stick. Cue. Whatever."

She arched an eyebrow. "Pool cue?"

"I don't know. I just know things up there got tenser than a Tennessean. Right before my eyes."

Loretta frowned. "Is that actually a saying?"

"Right before my eyes? Of course," he said indignantly.

Before she could respond, Little Jim came out of the elevator. "Loretta!" he bellowed, "My office. Now!"

The coach walked away, thinking Loretta was pretty stupid, and Loretta sat there, thinking the coach was pretty stupid. Loretta started rubbing her neck, giving it a precursory massage. She grabbed a fresh pack of Clorets from the shelf and got in tow behind Jim, leaving the checkout area unattended. The coach meandered to the back of the store where he found Tom, shucking corn with some of the new hires in the produce department.

"See, boys," Tom said, "Peel it down, and try to get all the fibres on the first pass. And all those sticky ones that just don't want to come," he added, "what you do is you grab the cob firmly with one hand, and give it a good brisk up and down with the other and use that friction to loosen the strings. Then you just pick 'em off quick." He finished shucking the cob, handing it to a sixteen-year-old kid who didn't give a flying fuck how to properly shuck a cob of corn.

"Yes, sir," the boy replied anyway.

"Coach Pecante," Tom said. "What can I do ya for?"

"So... did you know?"

"Know what?"

"Elvis leased Jim's old suite and renovated it. Little Jim didn't even know."

"You're kidding. Nobody ever gets anything over Jim."

"Under him, in this case."

"True enough. So, Elvis bought the box. So?"

"You've seen Jim's new suite?"

"Of course."

"You should go up and see Elvis's when you have a chance. Something's going on between those two. Something about a pool cue."

"Pool cue?"

"Mmm-hmm. Go have a look."

Coach Pecante left Tom and went to the battle room to prepare for the next day's game. He pulled up the competitors' profiles. One in particular caught his eye. It was the Thin Woman, who'd just finished her intense program of rehabilitation. Although he'd never met her, he'd seen her name and picture in the Sudbury Star news article, back when Horatio dramatically died. He wrote down her address, walked out of the store, and jumped into the yellow school bus. It burned ten times more fuel than his Hyundai, but since it was Jim's gas, he didn't particularly care. He drove out of the bad part of Hanmer, through the good part of town, past what any sensible person would consider part of the town at all, until he reached the Thin Woman's wreck of a house.

He went up the wooden ramp, one creaking plank at a time. Each board sank precariously with every footfall. He came to the landing and knocked. The door swung open. The Thin Woman stood there with a cigarette dangling from her lips. He could hear her kids screaming from within.

She looked him up and down. "The fuck you want? Little Jim send you?"

"I came to talk you out of tomorrow. It's not going to end well."

"Oh?" She took a nice, long draw from her cigarette. She held her breath, stared at the coach for a few seconds, then blew the smoke in his face.

He held his breath and waited for the smoke to clear. "Charming."

"Why wouldn't I run? What do I have to lose?"

"What do you have to lose? Are you joking? How much rehab did you just endure? Do you really want to go through that again?"

"Fuck you." She scowled and took another puff of her smoke, but diverted the exhaust inside her house this time, away from the coach and into the lungs of her children and disabled mother. "It won't be like last time. This time I'll have a helmet, and good shoes, and elbow and knee pads, and there'll be two-hundred and forty-nine other people to chase. And this time, that piece of shit lunkhead won't be there to stop me."

"And if you don't make it? Say you get taken down and break all the bones you just mended. What then? You go on the news and make a big stink about it?"

She shrugged. "Then I fall down. And everyone laughs. And we don't eat. What else is new? How many fucking times do you think I've fallen down in my life? Look around you, mister."

The coach nodded. He heard a child coughing inside. "You shouldn't smoke in the house with children in there."

She shoved her middle finger in his face. "See you tomorrow, asshole, mmmkay? Our groceries are on LJ this week."

"We'll see about that." He walked back to the bus and got inside. He yelled out the window, "You make me sick." He put the bus in reverse, easing it towards the road.

The Thin Woman stayed at the door, hyperextending her middle finger as much as she could muster.

The coach yelled, "Don't say I didn't warn you!"

She steadfastly held that finger aloft, smiling throughout the coach's departure.

-16-

J im usually liked game days. Not that he liked the game, mind you. He just really cared for the profits they pulled in. He'd been getting texts from his sister, accusing him of being too harsh on Jesse. Little Jim had learned long ago that sometimes the best way of making a problem go away was ignoring it, and if family was the problem, so be it.

He hadn't anticipated the Canadian teams doing so poorly in the U.S. market. He still didn't particularly care, provided revenue came in from somewhere. Having a finger in all the pies took care of that. What really irked Jim was that he'd let Elvis get to him.

Sitting on his spire balcony, he gave his head a good shake, then pressed a button on his chair, activating the intercom. Inside the store below, a voice bellowed over the intercom: *Jesse McGee, report to the spire balcony.*

The entire team was out in the back loading zone, getting ready for the day's game. Practice consisted of one bag boy taking a cart, running it up to speed, and letting go. Then another bag boy tackled it. Sometimes, a bag boy would put on sunglasses and walk around with a cane, making himself an obstacle that the other bag boys needed to avoid. It was all pretty technical stuff. The bag boys were all keeping their distance from Jesse, not letting him play in any of their bag boy games.

Loretta didn't mind that the bag boys hardly ever bagged

groceries, particularly after she reamed one of them out for crushing someone's eggs with a watermelon. It hadn't been the first time, it wouldn't be the last time, and the nice thing about having self-checkout machines was that when people crushed their own shit, they usually didn't come complaining to her about it.

One of the stock room employees leaned out the cargo port and yelled, "Hey, Jesse. LJ wants to see you. Now. Up above."

Jesse left the rest of the bag boys and headed to the elevator. Horatio accompanied him. Jesse hopped in and pressed the button for Jim's suite.

After a short ride, the elevator stopped unexpectedly at the lower suite, and the doors opened upon a smiling Elvis, cue in hand. "Hey, Jesse."

"Hello, Mister Elvis."

Elvis laughed. "Elvis is fine, Jesse. Just Elvis." Although Elvis and Jesse had spent quite a bit of time together at the pizzeria on game nights, the "togetherness" of that time generally consisted of Elvis sitting in his El Camino out back, baked off of his ass from cannabis-infused calzones. Elvis got in the elevator with Jesse. "You know, a lot of people are talking about what you did at that game."

Jesse didn't reply.

Elvis, looking himself over one last time for his inevitable showdown, noticed that his shoe had come untied. "Hold this, kid," he said, handing the cue to Jesse. He knelt down to tie his laces, and continued, "A lot of people are just bitter. They hate you because they have to hate *something*. The alternative is hating themselves for what they are. Know what I mean?"

Horatio agreed.

Jesse wasn't quite grasping the concept.

"You'll know what I mean soon enough," Elvis confidently explained.

The elevator stopped, and the doors opened. Jim sat at the bar, drinking a martini that he'd made for himself.

Elvis took the cue back from Jesse. "Just think about it, kid," he said, stepping into the suite. Jesse followed closely behind.

"Elvis," Jim said, "If you came looking for a game, sorry, but I'm not interested at the moment. Jesse — go wait on the balcony for me."

Jesse did as he was told, heading out the glass doors.

Jim turned to Elvis. "I'd offer you a drink, but I'm not sure if I'd get that screwdriver to your liking without a professional bartender. It's a shame that I don't have one. Listen, Elvis. I don't know what this is all about. This irrational anger. And after everything I've done for you."

Elvis was outraged. "*Done for me?* What about everything I've done for *you*, little man?" He pointed his cue at the table. "Nine ball. First to seven games takes the cue forever, fair and square. Winner breaks after each game. Lag for first break."

"I don't have time for this. I have to talk to Jesse. I'll deal with you after. Stay here." Jim went out to the balcony, where Jesse waited. "The rest of the team came to me, Jesse. Hektor started a petition. They all signed it. They don't want you on the team anymore. Not now. Not in the playoffs. Not ever. Not after what happened. But don't worry. We'll find a place for you. Uncle Jim's got your back, okay?"

Jesse shrugged indifferently.

They both went back inside the suite. Jesse started walking towards the elevator, but Jim stopped him. "Actually, Jesse, stay up here for a bit. I want you to see this. Your first new duty shall be to bear witness." He turned and pointed at Elvis, adding, "And you? *You* asked for this. I don't know what the hell your problem is." He stepped behind the bar and knelt down, grabbing something from the bottom shelf. He pulled out a tiny black suitcase-style cue case, and opened it.

Elvis started laughing at the plain-looking cue within. "A sneaky Pete? Really? Look at the size of that thing. Where'd you find it, in a Cracker Jack box?"

Jim clenched his jaw but didn't say a word in return.

Jesse stood there, incredibly confused.

Elvis added, "That thing is so small. It's smaller than my jump cue. It's tiny. Just like the rest of you."

Jim finished screwing the cue together, and slammed the case shut. He smirked. "You know what, Elvis? I liked you. I liked you a lot. I did more for you than anyone ever had before, or since. I guess with the way you've been acting, I knew it was going to come to this, but until now I hadn't planned on taking any pleasure in it. Now I'm going to enjoy every moment."

Elvis, refusing to be upstaged, doubled-down. "You know what? No need to lag. You can break. Then you can't say I didn't give you a leg up."

"Well, that's mighty kind of you," Jim said sarcastically, walking to the end of the table. He racked his own set, using his tiny nimble fingers to order and force the balls together nice and tight. "Don't... mind... if... I... do," he said with confident authority. He leaned his little cue against the table and grabbed a cue from the rack — a beautiful Balabushka, old and worn. Elvis cringed a little inside, watching Jim use the priceless cue to break. In Jim's hands, it looked like a telephone pole. He sidled up to the table in a wide stance and took a mighty stroke. The rack exploded, balls scattering. The two-ball dropped into the left side pocket; the seven in the far-right corner.

Elvis watched in horror as the nine-ball slowly rolled towards the corner nearest him, propelled by a lucky ricochet off the six. The nine turned end over end, settling half a rotation shy of the pocket. Elvis breathed a sigh of relief. Unfortunately, he was so focused on the nine-ball that he didn't notice the cue-ball and one-ball line up for an easy combination on the nine.

But Jim sure did. He'd seen it coming the entire way, preparing to take the shot (should it need to be taken) before the balls had even stopped moving. Once they settled, he took a quick stroke, delivering the cue-ball into the one-ball which in turn collided with the nine: a yellow-on-yellow impact that dumped the nine into the pocket and instantly put Elvis down a game. Jim stayed in perfect form, leaning over the table, the tiny cue bridged between his tiny fingers. He smiled, stood up tall, and strode around the table to retrieve the sunken balls for the next rack. "One."

Elvis scowled. "It was luck. Lucky break."

"Maybe," Jim said. He grabbed the Balabushka and broke again. Then he ran the table. And the one after that. Every so often, Jesse would say things like, "Nice!" or a subdued "Wow." It was an impressive show of masterful shots. Four games flew by. Then five. He sunk the nine-ball on the break in the sixth. Elvis watched it all happen. He held his cue, waiting for a chance to get in the action. Jim broke his seventh rack, sinking the three and eight balls. The cue-ball settled in a cluster with the five and four balls, hooking him. He had no play on the one-ball, which was sitting pretty in the middle of the table. "Push," Jim said, electing to play a safety. Jim tapped the cue-ball gently, rolling it less than an inch – enough that the edge of the five-ball was still *just* in the direct path between the cue-ball and the one-ball.

Elvis now had the opportunity to take the shot, or hand back control of the table to Jim. So, he stood up and looked at the situation. Analyzing it. Scrutinizing it. He crouched down, stood up, saw the layout from every angle. He could *imagine* the shot. See it clearly in his head. He couldn't jump the five-ball, because the four-ball was in the way behind it. He needed to swerve around the five. Hard punch. Perfect english. Flawless weight. Connect with the one-ball and drop it in the corner. He'd made shots like that before, when he had no other choice. He licked his lips. It was a hero shot. One in fifty at best. One in ten that he even made contact with the one-ball. If he took the shot and missed the one-ball completely, or hit the five first, he'd foul, Jim would get to relocate the cue-ball anywhere on the table he liked, and the match would be as good as finished. Elvis took a deep breath. He positioned himself to make the shot. Focused on it. He bit his lip. His pulse quickened. The cue trembled ever so slightly in his hands. *One in fifty*, he reminded himself. You don't go all-in on a one-outer. Especially when the cards are running bad. *Play smart*, he told himself. He looked over at Jim.

Jim smiled and shrugged. "Tough shot."

Elvis, at a barely audible level, said, "You shoot it," and walked back to his stool where he sat down with a thud.

Jim said, "That's probably the smartest decision you've ever made." He looked the shot over again, and imagined all the same things that Elvis had. Then he executed what he imagined. He punched the cue-ball hard. It lurched forward and to the side with sharp english, taking a tiny detour to skirt around the five-ball before straightening out and hurtling towards the one-ball, striking it clean into the corner pocket. The cue-ball bobbled back and forth around the table until it came safely to a stop. Jim quickly dispatched the rest of the balls in order, walked by Elvis without looking at him, opened the tiny case, and put his tiny cue away. "Sometimes even the smart choices don't pan out, Elvis. Harsh way to lose. Sorry."

Elvis said nothing. He looked at the floor, unsure of anything, feeling everything.

Jim went to mix himself another drink. "I'm not such a bad guy, Elvis. I thought you'd figured that out. You have the nerve to talk about what *you've* done for *me*? I could have found any fucking clown to shill shitty pizza! The Pizza Pi! franchise is a miniscule part of what I've created." He took a sip of his fresh martini. "I just saw another hard-working guy and thought I'd cut him a break. Maybe I thought we could be something symbiotic. But you seem to think I'm some sort of parasite! You know what? I'm still going to let you keep playing with *my* cue. Take it back down to your little den."

Elvis stood from the stool and began striding quickly towards the balcony, cue in hand. The doors parted, making way.

Jim had an inkling of what was on Elvis's mind, quickly swallowed what was in his mouth, and shouted, "Don't! The lot is FULL of people!"

Game days always brought out the crowds: people dressed like bunnies and dolphins, people in cosplay, and people dressed as anything else they thought might catch a drone's eye. The drones buzzed about, taking in reams of footage to splice into the pre-game spectacular. Elvis ran right up to the railing and hurled the cue like a javelin.

Below, a drone hovered in front of one the contestants. She wore a super-skimpy sailor costume, and bobbed organically in front of the drone, excitedly shouting, "I'm gonna run so fast, I'll be like the wind!" She blew air noisily at the drone. "Then

I'm going to blow past everyone, and leave the stampede in the dust! Whoo!" Then the shaft of the blue Falcon impaled her chest, lodging midway. Her eyes went wide as she looked down at the foreign object. Then she collapsed, blood gushing out of both sides of the hole.

The screams could be heard all the way up in the spire. Jim calmly watched Elvis, peering over the top of the balcony. Jesse ran out the balcony doors to see what was happening below. Jim just sat there, sipping his martini. He had a lot to think about. Drones quickly closed in on the balcony to get close-ups of Jesse and Elvis. Elvis looked pale.

Horatio left Jesse momentarily to go witness the chaos.

The contestants that hadn't run off the property were quickly forming a giant ring around the dead girl. From above, Jesse watched the doughnut of people jostle and move about in a wave. The bullseye of blood spread wider by the moment. There was something hypnotic about it all.

Horatio returned to Jesse. "It's bad," is all he managed to say.

Elvis slowly turned away from the cameras and walked back inside.

Jesse stayed on the balcony, staring at the ants below.

Horatio observed Elvis and Little Jim in the suite.

Elvis said, "I've never seen anyone shoot like that. Ever." He slowly shook his head. "Never seen it. Can't even be real." He shuffled over to the bar and sat, keeping two stools between himself and Jim. "I didn't see that coming. Nope. Just didn't see it. Who the hell taught you to shoot like that?"

"Well, in all fairness, Elvis, I never saw *this* coming, either. You've left me in a real jam here."

Elvis leaned over the bar, stretching his long body and limbs to the limit, grabbing the first thing within reach that would get him suitably drunk. This happened to be a bottle of forty-year-old Canadian Club whiskey. He cracked the seal and began taking steady, healthy sips. The cameras peered through the glass, observing everything.

Jim heard the sirens in the distance.

Elvis took a break from the bottle to say, "You didn't answer my question. Who taught you to shoot like that?"

"Is that really the question you want to ask right now?"

Elvis took another drink. "Yup."

"No one taught me."

"Bullshit," Elvis said. "Someone had to have taught you."

"My dad had a table. Old piece of shit. The cloth was faded and torn."

"So, your dad taught you to play?"

Jim sipped his martini. "You never fucking listened to anything I said, ever, did you? I just told you, I taught *myself*. He couldn't play for shit. If he'd been any good at it, he'd have cared for the fucking table better than he had. I didn't exactly have a lot of friends growing up. Hardly any toys. But I had that table and twelve balls to shoot."

"Twelve balls?"

"Well, the fourteen, nine, one, and the cue-ball had all vanished by the time I was old enough to see over the edge of the table. So, I played nine ball with the two, three, four, five, six, seven, eight, ten, and eleven balls, and broke with the fifteen."

Elvis felt a little bad for Little Jim. He sipped from the bottle and contemplated things.

Jim continued, "I realized a long time ago that pool was never a two-man game, anyway. After you've busted the rack, there's a beautiful randomness. The result is always something you've never seen before. A new puzzle to solve. When you're at the table, the only person you're competing with is yourself. It was never about the cue, Elvis. Sometimes it's just nice to have an opponent."

Horatio and Elvis both listened to Jim's words. Horatio thought deeply about them, considering the implications of chance in any given outcome. For one moment, Horatio understood Jim.

Elvis wished he'd taken the goddamned shot. He began fixating on that thought more than any other. He'd fixate on it until the day he'd die.

The sirens were coming from the parking lot.

Jesse, alone on the balcony, watched the paramedics vainly try to restart a skewered corpse. Then he saw the cops sprinting through the crowd.

Elvis began wobbling in his stool. He'd quickly polished off the bottle of fine Canadian whiskey.

Jim sighed. "That was a good bottle of rye."

"Bill me for it." Elvis softly laughed to himself. Then he stopped laughing, fighting to keep down the forty ounces of premium liquor.

The elevator arrived bearing two police officers.

Jim immediately pointed to the balcony. "He's out there, officers. I don't know what came over him. I... I just don't know."

Horatio screamed at Jim, calling him every curse word he knew.

The first officer, a short, stout, no-nonsense looking man with a thick moustache, looked outside, and nodded. "Huh," he said. "I guess this shouldn't come as any surprise."

The second officer, a tall, fit, long-haired brunette, sneered. "Figures. Big Jesse-fucking-McGee. I lost a week's pay when he got the Hares disqualified."

Jim said, "That's my nephew you're talking about, officers. Let's not forget that."

The officer quickly kowtowed. "Sorry sir," she said. "I didn't mean to be disrespectful."

"It's okay. But no matter what he's done, I love that boy."

The officers briefly looked at one another, tipped their heads in unison, then headed towards the glass. The doors opened, they walked out, and put the boy in cuffs. Jesse didn't resist. He may not have been the sharpest, but he knew what had just happened — and he knew what was happening now.

Horatio said, "I'm so sorry, Jesse."

The officers took Jesse into the elevator and disappeared.

Little Jim turned to face Elvis. "Get the fuck out of my sight. Go get some coffee. Go puke if you have to. Sober your sorry ass up. You're still leading the team out before the game."

-17-

Jim sat on his throne, trying to salvage something of the day. A less stubborn person would have cancelled the game. Footage of Jesse being escorted away in cuffs was all over the internet, driving up stream subscriptions for the event. Jim pulled some strings and arranged to have Jesse out on bail the moment they'd finished processing him — provided he stayed under his uncle's supervision at all times. A pair of drones followed his nephew everywhere. Jim contemplated the bad break before him. He'd planned on unveiling the new attraction after the game. Now, he wasn't sure if it was the right time. His network had been broadcasting the promo all week before and after every commercial break: *And don't forget to stay tuned for the premiere of MERCY! following The Cart Massacres!*

Jim went down to the parking lot. Paramedics had long since hauled the corpse away, leaving a red sticky splotch on the blacktop. The influx of costumed contestants had returned, and registration continued as normal. People kept a wide berth around the stain.

Jim went back into the store to find Jesse, freshly returned from the police station. "You. Go outside and clean up that bloody mess. Then go wait for me on my balcony. I'll be up shortly. We'll sort all this out Jesse, don't worry. It just had to be this way. I'm running out of options and right now, I need everyone on task."

Jesse walked outside, pushing a rolling mop bucket by the

handle of the submerged mop. His drone entourage followed him. Everyone outside booed. Horatio stuck by his side, though he didn't know what to say as he watched Jesse scrub sticky resin off the pavement while people hurled insults. Jesse wrung the mop out and pushed the bucket back into the store while Horatio and the drones followed.

Above, Little Jim stepped off the elevator into Elvis's suite. Bruce was standing behind the bar, ready to serve. Not that his only customer was ready to drink. Indeed, Elvis was asleep on his pool table. A puddle of drool trickled from his mouth, staining the felt.

Little Jim asked Bruce, "How much booze did you give him?"

"Not a drop, sir. He came down here, stumbled around a bit, then crawled onto the table. He muttered something about needing a couch in here. For the bitches."

"The bitches?"

"His words. Not mine. Then he said not to let anyone wake him for eternity."

"I don't have time for this," Jim muttered. "Get him awake. Force a gallon of coffee down his throat. Actually, make him puke first."

"With all due respect, Mr. McGee, you aren't my boss anymore."

Little Jim nodded. "I'll pay you two-and-a-half times what I was originally paying you to work for me again."

The boy smiled brightly. "Well, why didn't you say so in the first place, sir? I'll have him up in a jiffy." Bruce sprinted around the bar to the pool table and slowly rocked Elvis back and forth like a beached whale. Elvis moaned his disagreement. Bruce rocked him faster until Elvis turned onto his back, one arm dangling over the side of the table. Elvis started coughing, then settled again. Bruce hopped up on the table and knelt over Elvis. "Sorry about this, sir." He punched Elvis in the gut as hard as he could.

Elvis's eyes went wide. First, he clutched his middle. Then he tried to clutch his mouth, but it was a futile effort. He started puking up bile and rye. He quickly rolled onto his side. The table soaked up most of the wretch, with his shirt and hair each doing their part, too. He started coughing violently and puked several more times. His spasms quieted in a series of dry heaves.

Little Jim nodded his approval. The boy really did do great work. "Make sure he's ready for tonight's walk of glory. Not a pretty hair out of place on his body. We've got to put on the show of all shows today." Little Jim left Bruce to his task and went down to the store.

Coach Pecante saw Jim come off the elevator and tried to get his attention. He still hadn't figured out if Jim knew about the Thin Woman being one of the competitors. "Jim, I have to tell you something…"

Little Jim walked past Coach Pecante without acknowledging him, pointed to Loretta, and commanded, "Now."

Loretta frowned. "Now? It's game day. Look around. Idiots in costumes shopping and checking out? Duh?"

"Now."

Loretta casually slid off her stool, grabbed a pack of Clorets from the impulse rack, and followed Jim to his office.

The coach laughed. He'd deal with things himself. He headed to the pre-game conference where a dozen journalists waited, buzzing loudly amongst themselves. When Coach Pecante walked in, the journalists immediately bombarded him with questions. The coach shushed them. "Now, listen to what I have to say first, and then we'll take questions. I want to be clear. I don't want to hear anything about Big Jesse. All that concerns me is this losing streak, which I intend to snap like a pea on Christmas. If any of you so much as mention what happened today, I'll toss you out on your ass."

A reporter with a plump red face wearing a fedora hesitantly asked, "Can you give us any hint about the special feature tonight? Mercy?"

The coach furrowed his brow. "Mercy?"

The fedora nodded. "Yes. TCMN has been running promos for it all week."

Irritated, Coach Pecante replied, "I have no idea what you're talking about."

"In that case, can you tell us if you have any thoughts on the odds line for the game? The Hares are coming in as a three-to-one underdog — on home turf, to boot."

The coach snapped back, "Now, just you remember, nothing's for sure until that last cart crosses into an end zone or gets brought down. And don't you forget — we were undefeated in the first two seasons for a reason. There's more to it than tossing on a pair of snowshoes when it snows. Sometimes the snow melts, and you need a good pair of galoshes. And sometimes it freezes deep, and you need your skates. You have to be prepared for anything." He began sweating profusely and leaned heavily on the podium. "This interview is over." He stumbled towards the door, suddenly dropping to a knee and keeling over. He lay there while reporters surrounded him, taking footage.

The same team of paramedics that had tried to resuscitate a pool-cue-impaled corpse earlier in the day came and hauled the coach away, in front of a bemused crowd of sports journalists.

Tom escorted the paramedics out of the store. Then he used the intercom to call up the spire for Little Jim. "Jim," he said, "Are you up there? The coach is gone. He had a stroke, or a heart attack, or something. They've taken him to the hospital. Someone needs to come and run defence. Jim?"

Jesse, who had just reached Jim's balcony, was waiting as Jim had asked. He overheard Tom's voice, and pressed the button to reply. "What?" Jesse's voice crackled back.

Tom replied, "The coach is hurt. He's been taken to the hospital. Get someone into the battle room to run this game."

"Okay," the crackle sputtered.

Having done his duty, Tom got away from the insane crowd in the store and returned to the back, where he rubbed down expired chickens with vinegar, rinsed them under cold water, dried them with Bounty paper towels, and repackaged them.

Horatio told Jesse, "I wish I knew what was going on in your head sometimes."

Jesse went to the elevator. When the drones tried floating into it after him, he swatted them away. The doors closed without them. Jesse folded his arms and turned his back on Horatio. When they got to the main floor, the doors opened to the chaos of 250 contestants filling carts and running them through the self-checkouts. People were far too busy to notice him walk to the battle room, where he booted up the system. One of the contestant's profiles was flagged. Jesse opened it and stared blankly at the Thin Woman's face.

A hundred metres above them, Elvis was sitting on a stool, slouched over his bar. Bruce was busily force-feeding him coffee, one teaspoon at a time. Elvis did his part, swallowing the offering, while he tried to make the room stop spinning. Bruce looked at his watch. He couldn't wait anymore and forced Elvis from his perch, helping him walk to the elevator.

"I'll take the stairs," Elvis slurred. He pushed Bruce away forcefully and began lurching down the steel stairs, 'round and 'round the inside of the tower, using the railing to keep himself upright.

Bruce followed closely. Anytime he tried to overtake his old boss, Elvis just swept him back with his massive arms, keeping Bruce behind him. They made it down just in time for the start of the game. The bag boys were standing by their exits, ready to pounce as the crowd outside counted down. Elvis quickly walked towards the front doors. The entire world was spinning. He stumbled and slammed into the doors before they had a chance to fully open. He stifled a retch, stood back up, and walked out into the parking lot, towards his pizzeria, since it was as good a place to strive for as any.

His hologram stumbled around in unison at all the other scheduled games and was superimposed onto every stream. Elvis was everywhere. And he'd looked better. The crowd counted down to zero, and the contestants heaved their carts forward. Elvis collapsed on the ground a few feet from the doors and began spewing out rye-flavoured coffee all over the parking lot. Several drones came in for close-ups.

Inside the battle room, Jesse intently watched the screens. The Thin Woman had loaded her cart to the brim and would have made herself a prime target regardless of her notoriety. Cell phones, tablets, hams, expensive chocolate and perfumes — not to mention thirty-three cartons of smokes; she'd maxed out all her credit cards. Jesse deployed Hektor to lead a platoon of six Hares to deal with her. The Thin Woman pushed hard through the pack of contestants, putting as many of them as she could between herself and the incoming Hares.

Hektor rushed past the other contestants, his six men in tow, target in sight.

Jesse screamed, "Don't let her get away!"

The Thin Woman looked over her shoulder. For a chain-smoking woman who'd been in a body cast only a couple of years prior, she hustled pretty well. But Hektor was less than twenty metres behind and gaining fast. The other boys weren't much further back. She reached into a grocery bag in her cart to pull out a large, mesh bag of marbles, which she tore open, letting them tumble out onto the pavement behind her.

Hektor did his best to avoid them, but there were just too many. He planted his heel straight onto a shiny blue one and went heel-over-head, landing on his back. His neck snapped backwards, his helmet cracked against the pavement, and he lay there totally still, wind and sense knocked out of him. The other six Hares didn't dare get near enough to her to let that happen to them. They slowly shuffled their feet through the marbles to avoid the same fate.

The Thin Woman began widening the gap.

Crowds around the world weren't quite sure what they were seeing, but those who paid for the show were certainly getting one.

Jesse frantically shouted into his microphone, "Leave Hektor behind! Fan out! Don't let her take you all out at once if she tries to do that again! Two of you come behind on her five and seven, and then I want a team on either side. Get a little ahead of her and sweep in. Don't get right behind her again!"

Hares quickly surrounded her. She reached into another plastic bag, grabbed a large bottle of cooking oil, opened it, and started sloshing it out behind her, and to her right, and to her left. She tossed the empty bottle on the ground behind her, and kept running.

The two Hares trailing her didn't stand a chance. They tried to creep through the slick, but both had spectacular wipe-outs. The four Hares on either side of her had to delay their attack while they went around the spill. The finish line was close, but not nearly close enough for her to outrun them. The Thin Woman had one more trick up her sleeve: she began pulling handfuls of jawbreakers from another bag and tossed them towards the bag boys who were trying to flank her. She managed to wipe out one of the remaining Hares on her left, then one on her right. The last two bag boys were holding steady, one on either side of her. She'd exhausted her supply of ammo.

The finish line was still sixty metres away.

Jesse watched the Thin Woman from eight different angles. "GET HER!"

Horatio watched alongside Jesse. "I don't know how it got this messy." He wasn't just talking to Jesse. He was talking to the Thin Woman, and to Little Jim, and to Elvis, and Tom, and Loretta, and Hektor, and Eric. To Mrs. Tannenbaum, and her daughters, and to Julian, and Brian, and to Coach Pecante, and to everyone else that couldn't hear him. Horatio began to reconcile, with great difficulty, that just because good choices occasionally led to poor outcomes, it wasn't an excuse to make poor choices in the hopes of good outcomes — or worse, to give up on making choices altogether. He came to terms with the fact that sometimes you already know the ending, but you still have to watch it all play out.

The last two Hares simultaneously rushed towards the Thin Woman. She waited until the last moment to make her move. Just as the bag boys tried to jump her, she shoved her cart ahead as hard as she could and dove forward onto her belly, flattening herself to the pavement. The two Hares collided helmet-to-helmet in mid-air above her, and both dropped unconscious onto her back.

"UMPH!" she uttered, under the crushing dead weight of two grown men. The cart continued along, coming to a stop mere metres from the end zone. She strained, pushing with all her might, and crawled out from beneath the madness.

Horatio grinned.

Jesse was stunned. He looked at his displays. There was no one else close that he could send after her. He watched the Thin Woman lift herself up, dust herself off, take a long look around, and walk casually towards her cart. The crowd at the end zone was going insane. They exploded into a frenzy when the cart crossed the line, surrounding her and hoisting her into the air. She embraced the moment.

Jesse began obliterating everything in the battle room, piece by piece. First, he put his fist through one of the monitors. He yanked it out, his hand dripping blood. So, he used his other fist, putting it through a second monitor. Then he flailed about, knocking all the other monitors down, kicking them, stomping on them, shattering everything into a million pieces.

Horatio watched.

Jesse kept smashing things until the noise caught Tom's attention. Tom had been busily slashing the prices on wilted vegetables. It was so much easier to sell rotten meat. Wilted vegetables looked so... wilted. He rushed into the battle room and looked around. "Jesse? What are you doing here? What the hell happened?"

Jesse was panting with blood dripping steadily from his hands. "She got away." He sat down in the small pool of blood, letting his arms droop to the floor. "I had her. She got away."

"Riiiiight," Tom said. "I'll be back. You stay here, okay?" Tom closed the door and gave his head a good shake. "Should have called in sick today," he quietly muttered, as he called for an ambulance. Then he took a ride up to Little Jim's suite, but Jim wasn't there. So, he went back down and went to Little Jim's office, banging on the door. "Jim! You in there? All hell's broke loose in the battle room! Did you send *Jesse* down to coach the game?"

A moment later, Jim flung open the door and poked his head out while Loretta dutifully hid beneath the desk. "What the hell are you talking about? Why the fuck would I send Jesse to coach the game? Where the hell is Pecante?"

"What are you talking about? When the coach collapsed at the press conference, I called up to your box and let you know you needed to send someone to take his place. You said you'd take care of it."

"Slow down, Tom. What are you talking about? I've been in here for at least the past half hour."

"You need to get to the battle room. Jesse's in there and he's bleeding all over, and everything's smashed to hell and back. I already called for an ambulance."

Tom led Jim to the battle room where Jesse was crying on the floor.

Little Jim said, "Jesus Christ. Tom, call 911 and tell them to send the police, too. I have to go put out some more fires."

Tom nodded. "Okay... what do you want me to tell them?"

"Say Jesse violated the terms of his release and he's not my problem anymore."

At that particular moment, Jesse was too far gone to comprehend anything. He just kept muttering to himself, "She got away.... She got away...."

Jim took one last look at his nephew, then walked to the elevator. He got in and pressed the button for his suite. As the doors swept shut, four fingers wedged themselves between the panels at the last moment, forcing the doors back open. Elvis stood there, smiling ear to ear. He stumbled into the elevator, bumping clumsily into Little Jim. The doors closed, and they ascended upwards. Elvis was covered in his own vomit. The putrid smell quickly filled the tiny box.

"Y'KNOW," Elvis slurred, "You're really not such a bad little dude." He slapped Little Jim's shoulder, hard enough to knock Jim off balance. "Y'KNOW," he added, "When I met you, you made it sound like you'd solve ALL my problems. You did. You really did. And you did. Y'know?" He laughed, and slapped Jim on the opposite shoulder, sending him off balance again. "Where we goin'? Noo. Nope, wrong floor." He reached out and stabbed at the button for the lower suite. It took three tries, but he eventually got it. "I gots sumthin' for you to see. You'll like this."

The elevator lurched to a stop. The doors opened, and Elvis stepped out ahead of Jim, who followed out of morbid curiosity. Elvis stumbled over to the bar and grabbed his binoculars. "Need deez..." He shuffle-stepped towards the balcony. The sun was setting in the distance. Elvis peered through the binoculars and began laughing. "See? LOOKIT 'ER GO!" He looked down at Jim, who struggled to peek over the edge of the railing. Elvis laughed. "Short little fucker! C'mere!" Elvis shoved the binoculars into Jim's tiny hands then grabbed him 'round the waist, hoisting him up.

Jim saw what he needed to see. He didn't need the binoculars. Smoke plumed from the blazing fireball of the original Pizza

Pi! location. *It's kind of pretty*, Jim thought to himself as he watched the pizzeria burn. Then he saw the ambulance pull into the store's lot. The paramedics had been there a lot that day. They rolled a gurney into the store and rolled it back out a few minutes later with Jesse strapped to it. The crowd booed.

"Y'KNOW," Elvis said, "I'm thinkin' wecun make this work. Do meh walk, all that. Mmmhmm." He stumbled backwards, landing awkwardly in his rainbow patio chair, Jim still in his embrace. "Muurrm."

Jim looked at his watch. "In twelve minutes, we're supposed to premiere the first episode of *Mercy*! I had it all figured out, you know. It's all in the pitch, right? You build a story. You push the limits. Bend them. Break them. If the result is betterment for all, what do the means matter? You skewed my pitch, Elvis. You, and Jesse, and all you other fucking nitwits. You skewed my fucking pitch but *good*. And now... well, I guess now it's all over." He looked at his watch again and let out a small laugh. "Eleven minutes."

"I'm sorry, Jimmy boy. I'm sorry for fallin' down during muhwalk. I'm sorry. I puked all over. I think one of our guys stepped it in. 'M sorry. 'M sorry, Jim."

"It doesn't matter anymore, Elvis. None of it matters."

"Aww, c'mon lil' buddy. Try me. Wazzup? Mebbe I can help."

Jim shrugged. *Why not*? He explained the format of *Mercy*! to Elvis — this took the better part of a minute. Then he explained why he had no choice but to go forward with it — contractual obligations and such. This took about another minute. Then he said, "After a day like today, *Mercy*! is going to go down in flames just like your pizzeria, and it's going to drag all our brand names down with it. This is going to be worse than Fyre Festival. I suppose I only have myself to blame. We're going to lose everything."

Elvis chewed up the details, feeding data into his barely-processing mind. Then, he did what he always did when he had a problem that he couldn't solve: He reached into his pocket, grabbed his phone, fumbled with it until he got the unlock password right, and called Eric. When Eric picked up, Elvis screamed, "HEY FUCKER! HOW YOU DOIN'? HEY, SEE IF YOU CAN FIX MY 'LIL BUDDY HERE UP, 'KAY?" He handed the phone to Little Jim, said "I gotta pee," and went back into the suite.

"Hello?" Eric asked.

Little Jim replied, "Hello? This is Jim McGee."

"I don't know why Elvis thinks I can help you. I don't know if I'd even want to."

"I don't know if you can, either."

There was a long silence. Jim felt the seconds tick away.

Eric said, "Well, tell me your problem. Is it that life seems to have taken a major dump on you today? I'm not sure I can help with any of that. I'm not the Doc Brown to your Marty-fuckin'-McFly, short-stuff. Know what I mean? And even if I can help — what's in it for *me*?"

Jim laughed. "I've got nine minutes to change the future. Whoever you are, if you can fix this, I'll give you a million dollars immediately and hire you on as my full-time consultant for a quarter-million a year for the rest of my natural life."

Silence followed. Seconds ticked away.

Jim added, "My time's running out, kid."

"Five million. And 5% of your net profit from all sources, for life," countered Eric.

Jim roared with laughter, nearly to the point of puking. "Hell. Sure, kid. Why not. If you can fix this problem in eight minutes, you've earned every penny. You'll be my go-to guy."

Jim explained the concept of *Mercy*! to the voice on the other end of the line.

-18-

Jim returned to his suite where Mrs. Tannenbaum awaited him, sitting in her wheelchair. Sitting is a generous word. It's more accurate to say she'd been placed into her wheelchair in a sitting position but had slid into a hunched pose with her head tilted viciously forward, mouth hanging open, and a steady pool of drool collecting on her knee. The league doctor, a tall, dark-skinned, broad man with thin eyebrows and a toothy smile stood behind her. He wore a white lab coat and carried a clipboard containing Mrs. Tannenbaum's medical chart.

Mrs. Tannenbaum's daughters were both there, too, in wheelchairs of their own. "Well?" one of them asked. "Let's get this shit on the road! We have a plane to catch!"

Jim nodded his affirmation to the doctor. "Go ahead," he urged.

The doctor waved at the nearest drone and smiled. "Ah, yes. Hello. Yes. Hi." He spoke plainly, though it was clear that English wasn't his first language. He looked down at the clipboard. "Ah, yes. Yes, yes. Today's first patient is Gertrude Tannenbaum." He looked up at the drone's lens and smiled again. "Oh, yes. Yes. Yes, yes, yes. Poor Mrs. Tannenbaum. Very sad. Sad, sad, Mrs. Tannenbaum. Legally blind. Deaf. Of advanced age. This poor woman. This poor woman, she is very crippled. Comatose. Very little hope."

He walked over to the Tannenbaum sisters and shook both their hands. "Yes, very compassionate. You are good women, good to your mother, yes. Yes. Sign here," he told them, producing a pen from the breast pocket of his lab coat. Both ladies signed. The doctor looked the document over carefully. "Yes, yes. Very good. This is all in order." He began rolling Mrs. Tannenbaum towards the balcony.

Paperwork finished and consent paid for, the twins wheeled themselves towards the elevator, destined for places unknown, bank accounts padded by Jim's cash.

The balcony doors swished open as the doctor pushed the wheelchair through. There were a dozen rough-looking shopping carts queued together behind Jim's throne. The doctor scooped the tiny Tannenbaum out of the wheelchair, carefully transferring her into one of the carts. He rolled the clanking cart towards the railing. Clank, clank, clank, it went. Jim walked to his throne and pressed a button. The railing slid aside and the catwalk protruded out over the parking lot. The doctor pushed the cart firmly down the catwalk. Clank, clank, clank, the cart said, until it finally reached the edge.

Below them, the crowd looked up anxiously. A large swath of the parking lot was cordoned off from spectators. The crowd chanted along to the stream's prompting: "TEN! NINE! EIGHT! SEVEN! SIX! FIVE! FOUR! THREE! TWO! ONE!" The doctor gave the cart a firm push, sending it over the edge. The world collectively gasped. Fifty metres below, a drunken Elvis watched the cart and woman fall past his balcony, not five metres in front of him. The cart tumbled end over end, flinging Mrs. Tannenbaum out of it, letting her take her own journey downward. She plummeted, her hospital gown fluttering in the wind. She hit the ground like a stringless marionette thrown against a brick wall.

Fifty-seven people in the crowd screamed like they'd just seen the most amazing thing that had ever occurred in the history of humankind. They happened to be the same fifty-seven that Eric managed to get a hold of by spamming out the following text to everyone on his contact list: *M2AF - Get to LJ's in under five minutes and cheer like maniacs when she hits the pavement. Ask no questions. A POUND of Jack Herer to ALL who heed! NO BULLSHIT!*

Those fifty-seven cheers tipped the scales of social conformity. The crowd, most of whom *wanted* to cheer, but weren't sure if they should, roared insanely, and everyone watching from home followed suit. One by one, eleven more hopeless souls all followed her down. Families of the fallen were well compensated. The crowd cheered unreservedly each time flesh hit the blacktop.

When the premiere of *Mercy*! drew to an end, Jim addressed a drone directly. He'd spent the duration of *Mercy*! thinking of what he wanted to say. "Well, my friends, it's been quite a day. In my defence, I can only say that Jesse is kin, and it's easy to overlook the worst in family. Rose-coloured glasses and such. And to address the reports of the original location of Pizza Pi! going up in flames... well, sometimes things just domino out of control. No one was hurt in the fire, and Energetic Elvis is sobering up. He took that poor girl's death very hard and was terribly distraught seeing Jesse be so careless with such horrific consequences. I want everyone to know, that girl's family will be well compensated, and they have my sincere, heartfelt condolences. God bless."

Some days, bizarre things happen in bunches. The day *Mercy*! premiered was just such a day. Luckily, things tend to settle into place after intense periods of chaos.

On the Flip Side:

On the other half of the coin, the day seemed *far* less bizarre, at least to the unassuming observer. But you — the astute reader — are not just some unassuming observer, are you?

Hanmer in that reality was still the little haven of backwardness it'd always been. Little Jim's Grocery Store was surrounded by broken roads full of potholes. The store struggled to survive, and Little Jim was still Little Jim. He kept Loretta busy on her knees, Tom busy on his feet, and all the cashiers busy with customers.

Jesse was still in the early stages of his journey to football stardom and the infamy that would follow in *that* reality, having been spared the instant, spectacular rise afforded him in *our* universe.

Elvis's pizzeria, still standing, was doing well enough to keep him smoking, drinking, and shortening his life one day at a time. When he sat in the lounge chair out back, he was spared the view of the spire in the skyline, having never borne witness to the shortcomings of our reality. He'd eventually die in that chair, drunk, full of leftover deluxe pizza, wishing he'd done more for himself. Many a human being would have been envious to achieve such a fortunate demise. To own a business, have a full stomach, and have grown up in such a place? To such an age? Yet, Elvis would leave unfulfilled.

The Thin Woman continued gathering carts, slowly but surely filling up the lot behind her home. On her death, the children would sell all the carts for scrap metal, knock the house to the ground, and liquidate the property.

And Horatio? Horatio had just begun his third year of studying physics. One evening, he had a sativa-induced moment of clarity — a vision that would consume him.

Back to Reality:

From chaos, order rises like the phoenix. Patterns form. Destinies are set. Despite the terrible conditions of the day on which *Mercy!* premiered, the launch was a total success thanks to Eric's intervention. Things actually played out in Jim's favour: the bizarre day of death brought a massive influx of new stream subscriptions. In short order, Eric was Little Jim's right-hand man, trading in his orange backpack and bright sneakers for a neat and tidy suit, sharp leather shoes, schedules, and endless meetings.

And Coach Pecante? Forty-five minutes following his heart attack, he woke up in the hospital screaming, "If anyone's got any tater-tots, hand-em here, potato-man!" He promptly had a second, more severe heart attack, then died. They buried him with his whistle. In determining which universe Coach Pecante had a better run of things, well, it's sort of a toss-up. The alternative universe's coach would spend many years stream-binging and getting fat on a teacher's pension, eventually dying of diabetes-related complications. Our universe's coach is very much dead, but he sure had an intense run towards the end, never to be forgotten. Particularly after the discovery of Brian's body, decomposing in hefty bags under his back porch.

The Hares continued a proud tradition of being the worst team in the league, year in and year out. Little Jim didn't particularly care, as *The Cart Massacres* became a smaller and smaller piece of his pie. *Mercy!* quickly became the highest-rated stream on the planet. People could literally feel their lives getting better with each impact.

Loretta finally retired from the store. Little Jim realized she was far too convenient of a distraction and let her go with a generous pension. He couldn't afford to get sloppy again. Following her departure, whenever customers had an issue with the self-checkout terminals, Tom was required to drop whatever he was doing and rush to the front of the store to deal with it. He didn't get paid any extra for the work but continued doing it mindlessly, regardless.

Big Jesse was deemed mentally insane and unfit to be tried for the slaughter of the girl. They threw him into a minimum-security asylum, where he'd spend the remainder of his days. Horatio kept him company from time to time. Jesse effectively went mute, spending his days sleeping, looking out the window, and putting puzzles together in the care facility's common area. He didn't have to worry about paying his rent anymore.

And Elvis? He'd continue fulfilling his contractual duties, being Jim's clown whenever he was called upon. He'd take his walks of glory, pose for cameras, and appear in the Pizza Pi! commercials. He bought a couch for his tower suite, and moved in. He'd stumble down into the store whenever he was hungry. It wasn't long before a customer snapped pictures of him passed out in aisle six, a half-eaten box of Oreos in one hand and a bottle of vodka in the other. Jim refused to let Elvis's inebriation taint the brand any further. Taking care of Elvis's needs became one of Tom's responsibilities. So, in addition to running the store and maintaining order at the self-checkouts, Tom was constantly sending one of his stock boys up with food and drink for the burnt-out blond bimbo.

The Thin Woman enjoyed a brief stint of fame: she was interviewed on talk shows, questioned about her storied history with Big Jesse, and even championed as a hero of what physical rehabilitation could accomplish when someone was dead set on enabling themselves. Then she was promptly forgotten by the world. She returned to her routine of being a naturally shitty person, taking grocery carts home with her.

This, as it turns out, wouldn't be a problem for much longer.

-19-

In the time of a few short years, Little Jim's empire expanded beyond his wildest dreams: 128 locations, *The Cart Massacres*, *Mercy!*, and Pizza Pi! were just the beginning. He vertically integrated as many of the products he sold as possible. "Fat Roman Emperor," the official brand of LJ's, earned a giant slice of the market. Plain Potato Ships were the very first product sold. They were potato chips cut in shapes of famous ships and starships, and came in a black bag with no logo, with *this* written on the bag in bold white text:

Once upon a time, a potato farmer had a bumper crop. He simply couldn't sell all the spuds. There wasn't enough demand — people would usually eat just one potato at a time. He discovered that by slicing them thinly, frying them in lard until crisp, and pouring salt all over them, people would gleefully eat several potatoes in a sitting. 'Twas a good year for the farmer!

Consume, you Fat Roman Emperor! Consume!

Little Jim bought up all the good farmland in the Greater Sudbury region to grow the potatoes and manufactured the chips locally, selling them at all LJ's locations throughout North America. The black packaging and stories became the brand's signature icons. Tales always began with *"Once upon a time,"* and always ended with the directive: *"Consume, you Fat Roman Emperor! Consume!"* And they certainly did.

Within five years, Little Jim streamlined *everything*. Using state-of-the-art robots running the most advanced artificial intelligence available, he was able to let go of nearly all the staff in all of his locations. One human per store remained to do what little work needed doing. Even this was superfluous: the jump in insurance premiums for having a fully unattended location made it cost prohibitive not to have at least one employee on site. Tom got to keep his job. He'd spend his days watching robots stock shelves, prep fruits and veg, and keep things cleaner than any human ever could.

It wasn't long before the level of mechanization and vertical integration at all major companies caught up with Jim's. The unemployment rate rose exponentially. Universal Basic Income became the norm for more and more people. And how could they object? For most people, it meant being paid almost as much money to sit at home on their asses eating potato chips as they had been to work as slaves all day.

Jim continued innovating, and converted all the carts into self-driving automated vehicles. The filthiest thing in his stores were his customers, so he decided to take them entirely out of the loop. Instead, they'd order online, his robots would fill the carts, the carts would drive themselves to the customers, then return themselves to the store. Roads didn't get any more congested with all the carts wandering about since most people didn't have enough money to go anywhere or do anything anyway. Getting groceries and paying rent and utilities was about all they could manage on UBI. If they wanted more from life, they had to work for it. For all but the energetic few, that seemed like a fool's errand. Especially when Fortnite was free.

The Cart Massacres continued, though it was merely a facade of what it'd originally been. People no longer filled their own carts. The game evolved for the times. Carts were prefilled with the same quantity of fruit, veg, and other sundries. The selection of goods covered the entire spectrum of the rainbow to keep impact colourful. People didn't pay to play anymore since they rarely had the means. Jim ran the games as a public service. The groceries were entirely free, provided you could escape with them. The groceries that remained on the ground after the games were fought over by hungry spectators, birds, and participants.

Elvis continued doing his walk of victory before each game, though the Hares hardly ever won. The Pizza Pi! franchises were doing less and less business. Many people were transitioning their diets towards veganism because they couldn't afford the once heavily-subsidized meat or cheese anymore. Not at true cost. The ever-increasing lease on Elvis's tower suite ate up more and more of his earnings.

Eric, on the other hand, flourished. He planned to use his stake in all of Jim's pursuits to keep his family rich for generations. He and Jim worked hard each and every day, generating ideas, keeping the money flowing, and the people fed and entertained.

Eric and Elvis rarely spoke or saw one another. Few people ever saw Elvis — with the exception of Mel, who eventually moved into the tower with him. They slept on the couch and kept the place in a state of total squalor. Occasionally, Eric and Mel would share an awkward elevator ride together. They'd remain silent, having hashed out everything worth hashing out the first time they ran into one another in the store:

"Why are you here?" Eric had asked.

"Why are *you* here?" Mel had replied.

"There's a future for me here," Eric had said. "Is there a future for *you* here?"

Mel shrugged. "He'll have me. You won't. I want for nothing."

At the time, Eric took it at face value. It was true. When she moved in with Elvis, the suite hadn't looked so appalling. But as the state of the suite degraded, so did the state of Melanie. Eric hated to see it, but he also knew that it wasn't his place to get involved. He was busy making a difference in the world. Jim wouldn't live forever and one day he'd be running the show.

Vertically integrating so much of the business led to an absolute explosion in Hanmer's population. By 2032, it'd outgrown Sudbury to such an extent that Jim used his clout and connections to have the Greater City of Sudbury de-amalgamated. Then they re-amalgamated the entire region as the Greater City of Hanmer. This pissed off a lot of people in Sudbury, particularly the well-paid municipal employees who were all shit-canned. Jim replaced the entire lot of them with a fleet of a thousand automated robots. They started fixing the roads. They tended the parks, the libraries, the museums, the pools, the arenas, the waste filtration plants, and themselves. The roads in Hanmer were getting better every day as the robots toiled.

The Greater City of Hanmer: Birthplace of *The Cart Massacres*, home of The Annual Cart Massacre Championship. Vertical integration hub of LJ's and all her subsidiaries. Mother of *Mercy*! — franchised throughout the majority of the civilized world. The once tiny town turned into a high-tech metropolis. Brilliant minds flocked there, fighting one another for the few remaining jobs worth doing.

The vast majority of the region's original inhabitants settled into the UBI lifestyle. While some of them adapted poorly, spending all their time in their tiny boxes and watching screens all day, others sought enlightenment, taking advantage of all that their freedom had to offer.

Jim looked from his spire at all he'd accomplished, Eric at his side. In the distance, several new high-rises were under construction. They dwarfed The Commissioner's Spire by many hundred metres. "I know I didn't build this all myself," Jim said. "It was all coming, with or without me."

Eric was confused. "You think this would have happened to Hanmer without you? Look at the skyscrapers, and the monuments, and the roads... This place was stuck in the nineteen-nineties for three decades."

Jim laughed. "No, no. That's not what I mean. For Hanmer, I suppose I can take a little credit. We've *all* come so far. Every time we transition someone to UBI, we reduce their footprint to nearly nothing, and we free them from doing something meaningless. It's less energy wasted on people wandering to and from jobs that don't need doing, or people trying to get a little closer to whatever shiny object momentarily holds their fascination. I don't need to be *in* the Great Pyramids to know what they look like. Being able to individually reach every corner of our own planet has been of great detriment to it. We've *used* the world to see it. Eventually, humanity will expand to other planets in this solar system, then to other solar systems. There will be far more of us abroad than here. All that our descendants will ever have of earth will be simulations of one kind or another. Only those who are both rich *and* ignorant shall maintain the archaic fascination with wanting to *touch* history. One day their kind shall fade away and we'll finally be able to concentrate on what really matters."

Eric nodded. "You never wanted to travel the world? You could even take a trip to one of the new habitats on the moon. Maybe one day you *could* go see Mars."

Jim smiled. "No. For now, everything I desire is here, beneath my feet. It's a better place than most. I have no need to hop around the world aimlessly. Even a boat ride on Ramsey Lake makes me sick to my stomach. Someday, I'll take my trip. But not yet. Not until the time is right. And where I go, it'll be a one-way ride."

Horatio absorbed all that Jim had to say. The man could wax poetic, but Horatio knew his filthy secrets.

"I always thought you hated everyone," Eric said. "I didn't realize you cared so deeply about the world."

Jim was genuinely taken aback. "You think I hate people?"

"I think *everyone* thinks you hate people."

Jim frowned. "I didn't realize people felt that way about me. Maybe I was hateful, once. A long time ago. But I don't hate people now, Eric. I just hold them to high standards, and they consistently fail to meet them. That's what I hate. The lackluster attitudes. The poor work ethic, particularly when most people still needed to work. If you're going to do a job, *do it*. People always had a choice. Even here, this store, back when we kept it full of employees — they didn't *have* to be here. Yes, they made the minimum. But they could have been making the minimum *anywhere*. They *chose* to make it here and be miserable. Their misery fuelled their indifference, and thus, their incompetence. You should love what you do."

"Do *you* love what you do?"

"I wouldn't be doing it if I didn't."

Horatio found the entire conversation trite and meaningless, though it did beg the question: Did the Jim from *his* universe love what *he* was doing, too?

-20-

On the Flip Side:

Horatio took off his VR interface, once again frustrated by everything he'd witnessed. He'd brought his infernal machine online less than a year prior. Countless times, he wished he'd never invented the damn thing. Seven years ago, during his third year of university, Horatio envisioned a lens constructed from a Bose–Einstein condensate kept perpetually in the state necessary to exert negative force. The theory was, if the lens was flawless, he'd be able to use it to scan through time and space of his universe with no more difficulty than a web browser scanning the Internet.

He obtained a research grant and set to work meticulously building the housing to contain the fluid at the precise optic angle and conditions required. It took six years, and his entire grant. When he first activated the virtual reality interface, he witnessed a world not entirely unlike his own. He scrolled through our universe as an uninvited spectral. After a quick observation of the Laurentian University campus, he realized that something wasn't right. Things were different in the Sudbury he was seeing. Automation had taken hold at an exponentially higher rate than in his universe. He watched robots serve the students in the cafeteria of the Great Hall. At first, he thought he'd miscalculated and that he was viewing *his* universe's *future*. Horatio watched someone use their tablet, which confirmed that the date was correct. He kept hearing talk of Hanmer. *The Cart Massacres.* He caught a commercial in the university's commons lounge for *Mercy! — Available locally at all LJ's in markets with friendly euthanasia laws! Stream it LIVE!*

The Sudbury of this other universe was crowded. And diverse. And unemployed. But things also seemed on the up and up. People were a little less angry at "The Man," because around there, they knew who "The Man" actually was. Horatio took the pilgrimage, scrolling off campus at a driving pace, heading up Ramsey Lake Road towards the distant Hanmer. When he got to the corner of Ramsey Lake and Regent, he noticed two things:

First — Science North, the local, family friendly museum, now doubled as an Ontario Lottery and Gaming (OLG) casino. The casino opened nightly at eight p.m. sharp after they'd shuffled all the kids out the revolving door. Patrons could even play roulette on the turtle's back. It made for contentious arguments whenever the turtle decided to move at the last moment, jarring the ball. Them's the breaks in Sudbury, baby. It made a truly beautiful venue. Gambling proceeds went directly to the coffers of the Greater City of Hanmer.

Second — Health Sciences North, the hospital in *his* universe, directly across the street from Science North, was no longer a hospital but an enormous luxury hotel with an LJ's logo affixed to the side. A giant skywalk connected the hotel directly to OLG Science North.

Horatio was plenty sure by this point that his device wasn't working properly, though he didn't see the harm in wandering about. He obviously hadn't achieved what he'd set out to do — but he'd achieved *something*. In this strange universe, his beloved hometown was being crushed by Hanmer, just as Toronto crushed Mississauga and all the other towns and cities surrounding it. Things were very odd. The downtown Rainbow Shopping Centre had been replaced by a modern, eight-story parking garage. He wondered if the original crumbling mall had collapsed or simply been torn down. He didn't necessarily want to know the answer. Things really picked up at the intersection of Notre Dame and Lasalle, where traffic flowed down a freshly paved and painted eight-lane highway leading north towards Hanmer.

Valley East was a completely changed place. He didn't recognize anything. Everything was built up: hotels, shopping malls, museums, theatres, high-tech industrial centres. It was strange and affluent but also filled with dense, modern rowhouses of locals who'd simply been caught in the wave of unemployment. A UBI wasn't so bad, particularly for those who'd learned to live communally and efficiently.

Those up-and-comers, the robotics engineers, the tech-sector geniuses, the communications gurus, the research and development teams — all of them flocked to Hanmer, where the money was good, and where Little Jim pulled up his britches.

Throughout his journey, Horatio watched as shopping carts drove themselves around, delivering groceries. He simply followed the empty ones back to their source, where he paused for a moment to observe Jim's spire. He needed to know what had happened there. He began scrolling backwards through time, rewinding the wheel of history on our universe backward then forward again, stopping here and there to discern what he could from the media on the many screens available to him, or the odd conversations he overheard.

He learned of his counterpart's death fairly quickly. He watched someone load up the Wiki for *The Cart Massacres*, and saw his name appear early in the sport's history. He'd been a bag boy whose death warranted a small paragraph. The Wiki noted he'd been killed in a freak accident when a tow truck cable snapped, slicing him in half.

He remembered the day he'd walked into Little Jim's Grocery Store to drop off a resume. At least, that's how *he* remembered it. *He'd* walked in, dropped it off, and *left*. Little Jim had never boomed down upon *him* the way *our* universe's had. *He* went on to other things. And Jesse? Even Horatio knew who Jesse was in *his* universe. He was the hometown kid that made it big. The Cardinals had just won their first Superbowl, and Big Jesse McGee's name was smeared all over the local media. A quick Wiki search on *his* version of Jesse confirmed that he'd never been employed by his uncle. Horatio listened to a sports podcast where Big Jesse said that once upon a time, after his failure at the CFL tryouts, he flipped a coin to determine his fate, and that had the outcome been different, he'd have given up football forever.

Horatio's fascination with this other place escalated to a secret obsession. He didn't dare tell his colleagues of the successful failure. Something had happened in that strange, not-so-parallel universe, and it involved him intimately. He travelled back to the days following Jesse's CFL tryout and found the moment of the coin toss. He watched the coin float up into the air... Suddenly, the VR system shut down.

Horatio quickly discovered the problem. He narrowed it down to the most miniscule flaw in the lens housing: a single atom out of place in the lattice, an irreparable nick in an otherwise perfect creation through which subatomic particles from the fluid were escaping. He concluded that the flaw in the lens, one single atom dangling askew, warped the lens *just* enough to deflect the optic onto that alternate universe. He could only postulate that the lost lens suspension fluid had crossed through the gap into the other universe. He pondered the implication of the exotic particles he'd introduced there but shrugged it off. The particles had a short half-life once exposed to oxygen and he considered any risk to be minimal. Thus, he set about building an additional mechanism to keep a constant, positive flow of fluid into the negative-force lens, so he could continue his observations uninterrupted. The repair process took a few weeks. Whenever he'd take breaks from the work, he'd research the other key counterparts from his own universe. Coach Pecante, Little Jim, the Thin Woman, Elvis: they'd all been unremarkable. It was so bizarre.

Once the device was operational again, he returned to the moment of the coin flip. From there, he followed Jesse's path until it intersected with his own. Horatio watched a relationship blossom. He witnessed his counterpart empathize with the steadfast, dim-witted giant. They were two lonely bag boys, sticking together in a lonely bag boy world. He watched it like a highlight reel, stopping to listen when they were engaged in conversation, or when he saw one of them laugh, or cry. He came to understand them. He eventually reached the point when Jesse chased down the Thin Woman. He watched her hit him with the can of Chef Boyardee. As the other Horatio helped Jesse to his feet, for just an instant the voyeur Horatio swore that Jesse caught his eye — he looked *straight* into Horatio's point of observation.

Shortly after that, Horatio bore witness to his counterpart's death — his own, but for the tumble of a coin. He couldn't help but continue watching Jesse, knowing the boy would be so abused by Little Jim. Over the course of that first year, Horatio would turn on the device and make frequent visits. Sometimes, he was sure that Jesse could sense him. He'd often talk out loud, to see if Jesse could hear him. A silly prospect, if ever there was one. Yet, there were times that Horatio was positive that Jesse was looking right at him.

Horatio had a burning question he needed answered. Was *his* universe's Jim of the same mindset as the other, or had the other's mindset been corrupted by the opportunities placed before him? The drive from the Laurentian campus to Hanmer was slow going. Horatio fought the rush-hour traffic flowing out of Sudbury at the end of the workday, whilst swerving around several deep potholes. *His* Hanmer was very different from the one he'd been virtually spending virtually all of his time. Little Jim's Grocery Store's parking lot was in terrible shape. The carts... the poor carts. They'd all been so poorly treated. The inside was even worse than the outside. It *stunk*.

Wilted vegetables lay dormant. The meat was not fresh. The floors were sticky. Still, the store was busy.

Horatio approached Loretta, feeling as though he knew her. "Hello, I'm a reporter from Laurentian University's Lambda newspaper. We're doing a story about local businesses, and the pressures they face from outside competition. I was wondering if I could speak with the store owner?"

Loretta looked Horatio up and down while she chewed her gum. She summoned Jim to the front courtesy desk. Jim arrived, and Horatio repeated the lie he'd told Loretta. A minute later, Horatio was seated in Jim's office, looking down on the little man. Jim put his feet up on the desk. He looked tired and old compared to the version Horatio had come to know.

Horatio said, "Thanks for taking the time to see me."

Jim shrugged. "Not a problem."

It was difficult for Horatio to distinguish between the man

before him and the version he despised. He launched into the meat of the topic at hand — at least, the topic *he* wanted to discuss. "Tell me, Mr. McGee… do you love your work?"

Jim considered the question. "Well, the big players certainly haven't made it easy. I get by. My staff gets by. We take care of one another."

"That doesn't really answer the question, though, Mr. McGee."

Jim nodded. "No, I suppose it doesn't."

"Do you pay the minimum wage?"

"Of course. These aren't undocumented workers. I pay my taxes."

"That's not quite what I meant. I mean, do you pay anyone *more* than the minimum?"

"Only my grocery and cash managers."

"Do you think the other employees hate you because you pay them minimum wage?"

Jim frowned. "I should hope not. The job is the job. You don't sit at a poker table then complain about the blinds, the rake, or the rules."

"Do you hate them?"

"My employees?"

"Sure. Some of them? Any of them?"

"I'm hard on them. You have to be hard on your employees, otherwise they won't respect you or the job. But hate? No. If an employee isn't working out, I let them go. It's not emotional."

Horatio took a piece of paper from his pocket and said, "I'd like to read you a quote from the owner of a large corporation. He said, 'I don't hate people. I just hold them to a high standard, and they consistently fail to meet it. That's what I hate. The lackluster attitudes. The poor work ethic. If you're going to do a job, *do it*. People always have a choice. They don't *have* to be here. They make the minimum. They could make the minimum anywhere, but instead, they *choose* to make it here, and be miserable. Their misery fuels their indifference, and thus, their incompetence. You should love what you do.' Do you have any comment on that?"

Jim said, "I think I'd have to agree with that."

"So, then, you also love what *you* do?"

Jim mulled that over for the better part of a minute. He looked at his watch, then reached into a desk drawer, pulling out a chequebook. He wrote a cheque for $500 payable to the Laurentian Lambda newspaper, then handed it to Horatio. "For advertising. Whatever's fair and appropriate. Listen, son, I think that I've done what I've done because I had to. Someone had to. Every successful enterprise fills a need. I can't tell you that I didn't have dreams. I wanted to be an astronaut, you know. It never happened. It never will. But there are worse things you can be than an independent business owner. It's hard, frustrating work. At times it can be rewarding. My customers need me just as much as I need them." Jim reflected on his own words. "Now, if you'll excuse me, I need to get back at it."

Horatio nodded. "Of course, Mr. McGee. Thank you for your time." He collected the cheque that would never be cashed and parted ways with Little Jim.

Once Horatio left, Jim called upon Loretta, putting her to work one last time. The next day, he sold the store to Tom and left Hanmer to go on a worldwide tour, never to return. He would see and touch *all* of the history.

Horatio drove back to Sudbury and returned to his lab. He'd spent enough time in the past and the present of that strange other world. It was time to venture into the future.

Back to Reality.

-21-

C hange occurred exponentially. Few could keep up with the pace. Most of those who still had the chops to take career paths quickly burned out in the intense competition. People accumulated whatever fortune they were able before settling into the UBI lifestyle. Sometimes they worked into their forties. People working into their fifties were virtually unheard of. People like Jim were the exception. His robots swept through the land like locusts, repairing the roads and the buildings, erecting solar panels, and generally making life more livable for everyone. Over a period of five years, Jim upgraded all of Northern Ontario, bringing it to a level of prosperity envied by the entire world.

Then he set his mechanized fleet upon a new task. The robots began building sustainable factories, which, in turn, built more robots, which, in turn, built more factories. Jim orchestrated everything from his spire, rarely leaving its comfort. The robots multiplied in number. Each unit was fully articulated, dexterous, and deft at linguistic communication. They were capable of everything but *true* creativity, and would have made perfect stocking stuffers for every person in the world with the means to acquire one. But acquire them they could *not*. Jim would not permit their sale.

Beneath the toiling of those above, Tom kept watch over Elvis. It was the only thing left for him to do. Sometimes Elvis would ask him to play a game of pool. When Elvis wasn't *atrociously* drunk, Tom would take him up on the offer. Mel, usually intoxicated, would sit on the couch and watch. She'd cheer when Elvis made a nice shot. She'd cheer when Tom made a nice shot, which was rare. Nonetheless, Elvis would glance at her menacingly whenever it occurred. Outside the store, the world was constantly in a state of flux. For those three, stuck on the level between automation and genius, stagnation was the norm. Downstairs, the robots did everything, providing what consumers demanded, sending it out one cart at a time.

Little Jim, Eric, and all those who were driven and able to do so continued innovating. Ideas were there. What Jim lacked was manpower. His army of robots continued multiplying. In the meantime, Jim shoved his foot into the energy sector. The carts themselves, with their high-efficiency, high-capacity batteries, began off-loading energy to people's homes when they delivered groceries. This rendered rural power lines and the need to maintain them obsolete. Another decade passed. Jim and Eric found their fingers in every honeypot on the planet. The two were direct. Reasonable. Easy to deal with. All the while, the robots multiplied exponentially.

One day Jim told Eric, "It's time," and he let Eric in on his endgame.

The robots finally used the factories they'd built to create things other than more robots. They built small, interconnectable, mobile domiciles. The little boxes weren't fancy, but they were tough, soundproof, and made to last. They featured solar-paneled, flat roofs, and rain catchers running to a water purification system. They each had a small kitchen, sleeping area, and bathroom with a low-odour collection system — all the *requirements* of a basic life. They came pre-stocked with food, tools, and seeds for gardening.

The robots, one on each corner, simply carried the domiciles throughout Northern Ontario, setting them out in long strings. The homeless and underhoused flocked to them in droves, creating lives for themselves, breaking new frontiers, tilling new soils where climate change made it warm enough to tame lands previously untameable. Carts trundled along the interconnected roofs of the little boxes, delivering everything that the mass of human beings required, then hauling their waste away.

The robots built enough homes for *everyone*. Every Canadian, every American, every displaced person on the planet that needed a place to *be*, had a place to *go*. All they had to do was make the journey. Jim threatened to withhold the army of robots from doing any more public good if the burdensome Municipal, Provincial or Federal governments attempted to interfere with the incoming refugees. Offered the solution of a Utopia, and with the angry masses of the world watching Canada's every move, the multiple near-bankrupt levels of government were hardly in positions to negotiate.

And so, the people came.

Not all at once, but quicker than anyone expected, they *came*. From the furthest tip of South America, the wave of migrants exploded northward. They crossed oceans. They scaled walls. They helped one another along the way, for there was nothing to fear, and nothing to fight about. The people once burdened with turning those people away? They joined the flock.

The robots continued their work. Solar and wind simply weren't enough to keep the mechanized wave moving. Jim's army was limited by the supply of power available. They began the construction of a massive torus in the Canadian shield. Jim envisioned a fusion reactor that could create enough energy for generations to come. Some of the anti-nuclear crowd made a big fuss. They even staged an illegal protest at the construction site. The robots politely removed them, asking them to stay away from the construction site, which may pose a danger to fragile human beings. The robots scurried about, completing the project in mere months under the direction of Jim's science and energy divisions. Once fully operational, it single-handedly kicked out a thousand times more energy than all the hydro dams, nuclear fission plants, solar panels, wind turbines, coal plants, and gas plants on the planet combined.

Jim sat on his throne, Eric at his side.

Eric asked, "It's time, isn't it?"

"It's been time for a while. We'd better let Elvis know. I'll do it myself."

"No," Eric said. "It should be me."

"Very well. Make it quick."

"Just like that? *Right now*?"

"Do you have any idea how long I've been waiting?"

Eric nodded. "Okay. Let me grab my things. I'll go down and tell him, then I'll head out, too."

"Wait," Jim said. "I have something for him." He walked into the suite. Eric followed him in. Bruce was standing behind the counter, shining the same glass he'd been shining for twenty years. Jim said, "Bruce, hand me the cue."

Bruce bent down to retrieve Jim's cue from under the bar.

"No. Not *my* cue."

"Oh," Bruce said. "Yes, sir." He turned to the mirror at the backside of the bar and pushed on it, releasing a spring hinge. The mirror swung open, revealing a hidden compartment. Bruce pulled the blue Falcon from it, careful to hold it by the marble inlay. The wood of the shaft and the winding around the butt were stained in various shades of red. He handed it to Jim.

Jim promptly passed it to Eric.

Eric cringed. "What the hell is this?" He held the cue for a moment. "Wait. I've seen this before." He looked at Jim. "This is *the* cue." He looked it over. "So... you mean, Big Jesse...?"

Jim shook his head. "Nope. See that your friend gets that."

Eric was simultaneously shocked and impressed. Little Jim really was a hustlin' gangsta' after all.

Bruce bent down and grabbed Eric's bright orange backpack from beneath the bar. "You might be wanting this, sir."

"I'd forgotten about that." He took it from Bruce and brushed off two decades of dust. Then he walked around the bar, picked out a few good bottles of booze, and tucked them inside. He slung the pack over his shoulder and shook Jim's hand. "Never stop hustlin'. Good luck, you crazy old bastard. I think we have things well in hand now."

"Thanks, kid. You saved my goose. Without you, things would have turned out much differently."

"I did what I could. Thank you for the opportunity." Cue in hand, he started down the stairwell to go see Elvis.

Jim asked the oblivious Bruce, "Do you remember what I told you?"

"Yes, sir. I think so. The vacant lot where the pizzeria used to be."

"And all will be answered. You've been a good bartender. You make a good drink. I've put reference letters in your portfolio, should you ever need them, not that you should ever work for anyone else again." Jim shook the boy's hand. "Off with ya, lad."

Bruce grabbed his belongings, then took the elevator down. Jim went out on the balcony to sit on his throne, enjoying the view one last time. He contemplated the Hanmer he'd been raised in, and the Hanmer of his creation.

Below, Eric walked into Elvis's abode unannounced. Elvis was asleep on the couch. Mel was sitting at the bar, absorbed in a daydream. She looked underslept, undernourished, and underloved. She didn't even notice Eric walk up to her.

He tapped her on the shoulder. "Don't you ever go anywhere?"

She jumped off the stool in a panic. "Jeez, Eric! Why would you sneak up on me like that? What the hell do you want?"

"Pack your shit, it's time to go. Both of you."

"What are you talking about?"

"Elvis is months behind on the lease, Mel."

Mel laughed. "Whaa? What're you talkin' about, Eric? Elvis? Elvis! Get up! What the hell is this?"

Elvis groaned.

"Eric says you're behind on the lease? What is this shit? Eh? What're you talkin' about? He's rich. He's Energetic Elvis! Pizza Pi!"

Eric shook his head. "We folded Pizza Pi! eight months ago, Mel. We paid him out his share of the assets and cut our losses. He never told you?"

With great difficulty, Elvis rolled himself onto his side and sat up. His hair was a mess, covering his eyes. "Bastards," he muttered. "You stole everything from me. Traitor." He swept what little was left of his greying locks from his field of vision, and saw what Eric was holding. "What is that? WHAT IS THAT!?"

"This?" Eric asked, holding the cue aloft. "This is a present from Jim."

Elvis leapt up from the couch and snatched the cue away from his old friend. "I never thought I'd see this again. Why? Why give this to me now?"

"So you'll never forget, Elvis. Listen, I hate to rush things, but it's time to leave."

The rhythmic thumping of robots coming up the stairs distracted Elvis. "What's going on? What is that?"

Fifty robots came into the suite holding large, empty crates. The rhythmic march continued as more robots climbed up the stairs towards Jim's suite with fully loaded crates. The lead robot asked, "What are we taking out, sir?"

Eric said, "Everything. Disassemble the pool table and take it out of here. Go dump it all in one of the end zones. He can deal with it there."

The robots set about their tasks, efficiently solving the minutia of little intricate problems required to accomplish them.

Elvis yelled, "Hey! Would someone mind telling me what the hell is happening?"

Eric shrugged. "It's time to go, Elvis."

The contents of the room quickly vanished as the robots packed it away. Two robots walked casually past Elvis, each carrying one half of the slate from the pool table, hefting the slabs down the stairwell with no more difficulty than burly construction workers hauling sheets of drywall.

Orange lights began flashing and a siren sounded.

Mel began screaming. "Eric! What the hell is happening!? Where are you going?"

"Somewhere that isn't here."

She looked around at the situation, and at Elvis. "Can I come with you?"

Elvis held the cue menacingly, staring Eric down.

Eric nodded to Mel. "Of course."

Elvis sneered. "So that's how it's going to be, eh? My *friend*.

You stole everything from me! You're all a bunch of thieving bastards! You, Jim, his rat-faced lawyer. All of you!"

Eric sadly shook his head. "After all this time, you still think the lawyer fucked you? You can be so fucking dense, Elvis! As though a high-priced lawyer would pilfer your little cash float."

"He was the only one!" Elvis screamed. "No one else had access!"

"No one?"

Elvis's eyes filled with true rage. "YOU! YOU STOLE IT! THIS IS ALL *YOUR FAULT*!"

"I didn't *steal* it. I took it, and left you that premium bag of herb, remember? I thought you'd put this all together years ago. It was like two hundred bucks. You'd just walked into a fucking fortune."

Elvis tried to focus. "I thought the weed was a gift."

"Nothing in life is free, baby. How many times have I told you that? Why would you even *think* it?"

Elvis spit in Eric's direction. "You were *nothing* before me. NOTHING!"

The orange flashing intensified and the siren grew louder.

"Time to go," Eric told Mel. "You, too, Elvis."

Elvis stood his ground. "I'm not going anywhere." He grasped the cue firmly.

Eric considered the man before him — a man he hardly knew. "Suit yourself." He took Mel by the hand and led her to the elevator.

"Hey Eric," Elvis called out.

Eric turned around. "What, Elvis?"

"You're the most corporate bitch I've ever met. Never forget that."

Eric nodded. "Yeah... I know." As the elevator doors opened,

Eric said, "But it's hard to argue with success."

"Fuck you."

Eric and Mel left Elvis behind and shared an awkward ride down together. In the store, they found Tom panicking near the entrance, clueless as to what was happening.

Eric said, "Hey, buddy. Listen. Do you remember the combination to Jim's office safe?"

Tom nodded.

"Good. Go empty it, then run like hell. Take whatever's there. Be quick about it, and get to one of the end zones. Have a nice life. Your paychecks will continue to come."

Tom shrugged, nodded, and made his way to Jim's office.

Eric and Mel walked towards the vacant lot where the pizzeria used to be.

-22-

I mmediately after parting ways with Eric and Bruce, Jim sat on his throne and stared at an orange button on the armrest. He'd never pushed it before, though he'd thought about it many times. Times when he'd been overworking himself and wanted an out. Times when the public image of him wasn't as shiny as it was now. He took a deep breath, pushing it three times. Robots everywhere in Hanmer stopped what they were doing and came running towards the store. Some of them found their way up the spire, carrying crates of supplies from below. When the first of them reached Jim's suite, an alarm sounded and orange lights strobed throughout the building.

The robots disassembled the pool tables, the bar, and the fixtures, taking everything down. The booze, furniture, and the cues were all vacated. Two robots disconnected the throne unit from the balcony, moving it inside the suite facing the sliding glass doors, which the robots welded shut. They sat in the throne's side-chairs, where they waited patiently.

Jim sat down in his re-installed throne. "Everything's green?"

The robot to his left replied, "Yes, sir. Our brethren have evacuated all humans to a distance of five hundred metres. The one named Elvis refuses to leave of his own volition, despite the alarms. Would you like us to remove him from the suite by force?"

Below, Elvis stood on his balcony, clutching his stick. One of the robots tried reason. "Sir, you can't be here. You must leave."

"Why!?" Elvis demanded to know.

"This property is scheduled for termination."

"What the hell are you talking about!?"

"This property is scheduled for termination. You must leave the premises immediately."

Elvis thought about his past choices. He just didn't see how he could have changed anything. The sirens blared. Why hadn't he taken the fucking shot?

"Now, sir. You must leave!" The robot picked up Elvis as gently as it could, though Elvis didn't make it easy: he hit the robot with his cue repeatedly. The robot carried him as graciously as possible into the elevator and down to the store, placing him gingerly on the ground outside the front doors. Then it unceremoniously plucked the cue from Elvis's hand.

Horatio was watching. Jim was watching.

"Give that back!" screamed Elvis.

"This property is scheduled for termination," the robot said, gesturing to the cue.

"Termination? Property? It's *MY DAMNED CUE!*"

The robot shook its head. "I'm sorry, sir. My records indicate that this cue is the property of Jim McGee." The robot carelessly tossed the cue back into the store and looked indifferently at the human sitting on the ground. "Thank you for shopping at Little Jim's, sir. Please proceed to an end zone immediately. You are in imminent danger. Have a nice day!" The robot sprinted down the street.

The automatic doors slid shut in Elvis's face. Elvis crawled over and began pounding on the glass. "My cue! That's MY FUCKING CUE!"

Up in Jim's suite, five-point harnesses extended automatically from the seats, clamping down securely around Jim and the robots. "Not to worry, sir," the robot on his left said. "We've kept everything in good working order. Our brethren are dismantling the elevator and stairwell and installing the necessary components. However, Elvis refuses to leave the property. Shall we abort?"

Jim watched on the monitor. Elvis was busy trying to manhandle a straggling grocery cart so he could ram it through the store's doors. The cart was having none of it. It pushed Elvis to his ass, leaving him there while it made a hasty getaway.

Jim scowled. "No. It's time to go. This is as merciful as it gets."

"Yes, sir," the robots said in unison.

A thirty-second countdown began blaring over the speakers.

Elvis continued futilely trying to kick down the door.

The countdown expired.

Above Elvis, something began rumbling. He looked straight up to see his suite detach from the tower and fall towards him. Before he could even think about how to react, a powerful plume of fire gushed out of the back of his old home, pushing it away from the tower, past the front of the store. Elvis screamed and covered his head as it crashed spectacularly into the parking lot — an explosion of steel and glass versus blacktop, barely fifty metres from where he was sitting. The rumbling didn't stop there. It only grew stronger. Eighteen refurbished Merlin rocket engines came to life, lifting the entire tower away from the store, engulfing LJ's in an enormous fireball that vaporized Elvis along with his cue.

The entire city turned to look. A moment later, the rest of the world tuned in. The tower rose majestically into the air. Once it broke orbit, and the first stage's engines were exhausted, the bottom portion of the tower detached, falling back towards earth. The second stage's nine additional Merlin engines ignited, blasting The Commissioner's Spire towards the great unknown. The first stage of the rocket made a controlled re-entry, nailing a flawless vertical landing in the parking lot at OLG Science North, where it would become their newest exhibit.

Above, Jim held on for dear life while everything violently shook and rattled. When the engines were spent and quiet, the spire detached from the suite, leaving Jim and his robots on a trajectory out of the solar system. Thrusters on the suite reoriented it so the balcony window pointed back towards Earth. Jim released himself from his seat, floated over to the window, and waved goodbye.

-23-

M el and Eric ran to the corner where the pizzeria used to be. They found Bruce there, watching a swarm of robots in the process of erecting a small building, complete with the bar and pool tables from Jim's suite. The robots stocked the bar with Jim's booze, and erected a sign that read, "Bruce's Bar."

Bruce nodded approvingly. "Little Jim was all class," he said.

The three turned around when they heard a thunderous crash come from LJ's. Then the ground started shaking.

"Watch," Eric said.

In the distance, the spire began to rise. Soon, the entire tower was airborne, trailed by a massive plume of fire. A piece of Hanmer vanished into the sky.

"Where is he *going*?" Bruce asked.

Eric said, "Nowhere. Everywhere. He doesn't care where he winds up. He just wants to be the first to get there. His ship has enough supplies to sustain him for as long as he has to live. Then the robots will preserve his body in stasis. He's on a course that will take him through multiple star systems. His hope is that one day, long after he's dead, alien life may find him. The robots will acquaint them with humanity."

Mel nodded. "He's fucking crazy."

"No doubt, girl. No doubt."

On the Flip Side:

Horatio pulled off the VR interface and rubbed his eyes. He couldn't believe what he'd just seen. After a short lunch break, he re-entered the madness, fast-forwarding twenty years. In two short decades, innovation was only curtailed by imagination. Humanity colonized the solar system then prepared to colonize others. Although that future was *amazing*, it lacked the drama of Little Jim's era. Horatio found Little Jim well on the way to Alpha Centauri, and very near death. His robots kept him company. He even had a virtual, holographic pool table, but he was no match for those fucking robots. Sometimes they'd humour him. "Good shot, sir," they'd say. The ravages of space travel had taken their toll on the tiny man's body. He looked back towards Sol, his native star, took one last breath, and ceased his conscious existence.

The robots preserved his body, then took their seats flanking the empty throne. The robot on the left looked at the empty seat as though it was thinking about sitting there. The robot on the right looked at its counterpart, and they held one another's gaze for many seconds. The robot on the left asked, "Turns? You can go first. We can switch after every century." The robot on the right found this agreeable. Robots are such reasonable things. They continued their peaceful journey.

Horatio scrolled forward through time, watching the little ship travel out of the bad part of the Milky Way, into the not so bad part, then into the good part, through the better part of the good part, into the best part, and beyond. The ship continually broadcasted greetings over multiple mediums, hoping to catch someone's attention.

They would enter a planetary system, use the local star for

a gravity assist, and continue to the next one. Everywhere it went, it relayed all the data it collected back to Earth. 14,288 years later, after passing through seventy-three planetary systems, the little ship was engulfed in light and towed aboard a massive intergalactic space cruiser: the capital ship of a large fleet, tasked with protecting a swath of thousands of star systems and inhabited worlds.

Aliens of all shapes and sizes picked Jim's ship apart, piece by piece. They left one of the robots intact and dismantled the other to see how it worked. Then they put it back together, leaving it none the worse for wear. Horatio watched as two of the aliens began pointing frantically at the screen of a handheld device. They both started moving around the room. Horatio kept having to scroll out of their way. They kept walking in his general direction. Horatio stayed still. The two aliens stepped in front of his perspective and looked straight into the lens. They pointed the device right at it.

Horatio looked down at the screen on the device the alien held. He immediately recognized the subatomic makeup of one the exotic particles he was using in the negative-force lens. Alarms began sounding on their ship and the two aliens ran down a corridor. Horatio followed them into some kind of engine room. All the different looking aliens were panicking. Suddenly, the enormous ship exploded around Horatio, leaving him alone in the vacuum of space, surrounded by debris and alien bodies.

Horatio panicked. He scrolled backward, following the ship from where it came. He scrolled forward again. The aliens on the ship had managed to send detailed records of the brief encounter with Jim and his robots back to their nearest ally prior to their destruction. The incident ignited an intergalactic war. Humanity had managed to go unnoticed while colonizing dozens of worlds throughout dozens of different solar systems. Unprepared for the coming onslaught, the human race and everything it ever created was wiped out by the alien conglomerate. Horatio watched right until the end. When the last human colony was destroyed in the year 18,087 ad; the aliens celebrated the completion of the purge.

Horatio took off the VR interface, went to the bathroom, and promptly threw up. He went home, where he thought about everything he'd seen, and everything he'd felt. He went back to the lab the next morning and activated the interface. First, he visited Jesse in the mental asylum, the day that Jim left Earth. Jesse was huddled in a corner of his room staring at nothing in particular.

"This has been a monumental failure," Horatio said.

Jesse bit off a hangnail, chewed on it, then spit it out.

Horatio asked, "What would *you* have done differently?"

Jesse put his hands out, like he was holding a football in front of him. "I wish I could change things," he quietly said.

Horatio stayed there a while longer, keeping Jesse company before travelling back to the time and place that Jesse flipped the quarter. Horatio focused the lens on the apex of the toss, aligning the flaw in the optic directly over George Washington's eyeball. He cranked the pressure up on his compensation unit, increasing the flow of fluid into the lens housing to maximum. A mighty stream of subatomic particles escaped into that strange universe, the odd one colliding with the matter in the coin, pushing it ever so slightly, increasing its rate of rotation. It tumbled into Jesse's open palm, tails up.

ABOUT THE AUTHOR

J ohn Robert Cameron hails from Sudbury, Ontario, in the great wide land of Canada. If you enjoyed this story please seek out my other titles:

The Second Lives of Honest Men

The near-future is a dark place, at least according to Jacob Wentworth, a history professor near the end of his long tenure. When a prodigy student discovers the means to time travel, they ask themselves: Can a figure from the past bring sense to the present?

Enter Final Gamer

Eons from now humanity has spread throughout the Universe to its very ends, quelling every last star system. But the introduction of a prophesized wildcard puts all Utopia on edge. In this pop-culture-driven tale of Science Fiction, the only thing higher than the drama are the stakes.

SUPPORT MY CREATIVE VERVE!

Become a PATRON for insider access to my newsletter and more!

patreon.com/JohnRobertCameron

Follow me on Facebook and Goodreads!

facebook.com/EnterFinalGamer
goodreads.com/JohnRobertCameron

ONE LAST LITTLE THING...

Please, please, pretty please leave a kind rating on Amazon?

Better yet, would you take a moment to write a review, too?

Even a sentence or two makes a world of difference.

Just go to my author bio at amzn.to/3RXRlNh (Caps sensitive!)

Select this book, then scroll down, and click on "Write a customer review". You'll find it on the left, under "Customer reviews" & "Review this product".

You're the best!

Manufactured by Amazon.ca
Bolton, ON